THE GRAIL MAIDEN

THE GRAIL MAIDEN

E.C. AMBROSE

Cover art by Rachel Marks

Interior designed and formatted by

www.emtippettsbookdesigns.com

BOOKS BY
E.C. AMBROSE

The Dark Apostle Series
The Burning
Elisha Barber
Elisha Magus
Elisha Rex (Coming Soon)

WRITTEN UNDER THE NAME
ELAINE ISAAK

A Song for the Sea
The Eunuch's Heir
The Singer's Crown
The Bastard Queen

Tales of Bladesend
Winning the Gallows Field (Book 1)
Joenna's Ax (Book 2)

THE GRAIL MAIDEN

"And there, the knight saw such a vision, a vision of truth, of hope, of divine love," the bard said, glaring from time to time at the head table where the newly acceded King Edward II was murmuring to his favorite, Piers Gaveston, recently returned from exiled and granted the title Earl of Cornwall.

Lord Randall, seated with Prince Hugh between himself and the king's favorite, couldn't help but notice Hugh's irritation toward the new Earl, already supplanting Hugh himself as the new king's right-hand man. Randall himself remained close to the king primarily through his attachment to Hugh, making the whole morass of power and politics, already muddled by Edward Longshanks' death, that much worse. Hoping for a distraction, Randall cleared his throat and gestured toward the bard who tried so hard to entertain them.

"I speak of the Grail, my lords," the bard said, more

loudly, "borne in the hands of a lady more beautiful than any mortal maid. The greatest treasure known to man!"

"Au contraire," Gaveston interjected, his Gascon accent adding a lilt as he glanced at the king, rolling a gilt-framed oval between his fingers then clenching it in his fist. "I would say that love is the greatest treasure."

Glowering at the young king's favoritek, Hugh said, "Love—paugh! It is strength of arms a man should treasure. I have little taste for mere tales of daring—let us have deeds instead."

The bard's brow furrowed and he tugged at his tunic as if he'd like to wrap his hands around the throat of one of the inattentive nobles, then he managed a smile and struck a pose to begin again. "Perhaps a tale of love would—"

"Hugh, you've never been more right!" declared the king, thumping his hand on the table and stopping whatever the bard might have planned to say. "Deeds of arms are what we've all come here for, is that not so? To bring down the Scots, as my father—God Rest his soul—so longed to do."

"Here, here!" roared Hugh along with everyone else in earshot, and Randall, too, raised his cup, though he worried where this conversation might be leading. It was already October—rather late in the season to sally forth. Time, in fact, to be heading for their own estates and to send for the princess who was to marry their new king. But then, perhaps the marriage itself was what Edward wished to delay.

"It does sound quite an adventure," Gaveston offered, smiling a little too much, dropping the thing he had been holding to stroke his many-ringed fingers along the king's arm. "To ride against these ferocious Highlanders and show them a little of our English might."

Randall glanced away, his eyes flicking past the silently seething bard. Another tale of chivalric legend, or another futile foray toward the highlands — he would be ready for either, but he favored neither choice. Across the hall of Carlisle castle, the ladies gathered in their place by the great hearth, a cluster of vivid color and quiet talk. Allyson sat among them, listening, stitching, as ever, quiet and withdrawn from the others, as ever: a cold beauty he had once been proud to claim as his wife. Only two years had passed since the wedding, but it felt like forever. Then he noticed what Gaveston had discarded to take up his talk of adventure: an ivory miniature of Edward's intended bride, Princess Isabella of France, a robust young woman, dark-haired, bright eyed, voluptuous where Allyson was slender. They shared a similar distance, but Isabella owed hers to the waters and lands between the border of Scotland and the palace at Paris, while Allyson. . .no, even he did not know what set such space between them.

Randall reached out and took up the portrait. "Your Majesty might rather head for London and prepare to receive his lovely betrothed." He held it out at an appealing angle.

Gaveston sat sharply back, his mouth pinched, but the king merely laughed. "Have you no stomach for the fight? As well you might — myself, I have been occupied with matters of state while it has been left to men like you to bear the brunt. So, my Lord Randall, I grant you the honor of remaining at Carlisle, to guard my father's coffin until my return. One final victory shall give him a fine send-off to the Lord." He raised a goblet and twitched his eyebrows.

"Your majesty can't really mean—"began one of the older lords at the same time that a few of the younger ones cheered, and Gaveston clapped the king on the shoulder, flaring his eyes at Randall as if he'd scored a victory of his own.

"Edward, we should thank the good bard for inspiring such chivalry," Gaveston said, reaching into the king's own purse to flick a coin at the bard. "I've heard that Robert the Bruce, whom the Scots claim as king, is quite the worthy knight himself."

"Worthy?" Edward waved this away. "I'll grant you he seemed noble enough when he was a part of my father's court—when he pledged his loyalty and honor to his rightful king. God willing, he shortly shall be pledging it to me."

This earned him another roar and Randall joined in, but faintly. He pictured the powerful, courtly and battle-wise Bruce in combat with King Edward II, a lithe, unseasoned young man who, for all that he had a few years on Randall, still had hands barely calloused and preferred his garden to his garrison any day. Maybe Gaveston was right, and the ancient tales of Arthur did indeed inspire the young king. God willing, they would inspire in him some sense.

"If the rumors are true," said Hugh, glancing from Randall to the king, "then it might be a fair time to strike after all, in spite of the season. I've heard the Bruce is camped not far north of Dumfries, in support of his friend the black Douglas."

"That's barely two days's ride." Edward leaned toward his bastard brother, eyes keen. "I'll wager it was our father's death that brought him so near. He hopes to take advantage of us in our grief!"

Grief indeed. Randall had spent more time on his knees at chapel than Edward, who waited barely a week out of respect for the deceased before sending for Gaveston to be recalled from exile. He suspected, if Edward had his way, he'd have been toasting his father's death instead of calling for blessings upon his path to Heaven. As it was, he could hardly contain his exuberance now that Gaveston was here. The Scottish campaign, gone from hope to shock at Longshank's death, swung now toward farce as Edward presented the war as if it were his own, gallantly showing it off for his favorite. Since Gaveston's arrival, Hugh and Edward spent less time together, and he wondered if Hugh's pride provoked his support of the Edward's rash idea — Hugh could once again display his own prowess while Edward and Gaveston floundered on the field of battle.

Edward's face grew solemn of an instant, and he clasped Hugh's hand in both of his. "My friend, my brother, I cannot allow you to accompany us. Father would never forgive me if anything happened to you."

Hugh scowled, his blue eyes sharp, his features sharper. "Truly, your majesty, Randall and I would both prefer to be at your side, where we can best defend yourself and England."

"In faith, your Majesty, while I hesitate to reject the honor you've granted me," Randall began, but Edward shook his head gently.

"No, my friends, you shall not persuade me." He shook his finger at Randall, "And well I know you have the gift for such persuasion. But no, tonight, I am resolved! On the morrow, we ride out to find the Bruce!"

FOUR DAYS later, the hall half-empty of knights and without its fresh young king sounded hollow to Allyson's attentive ear. More attentive, in fact, than any of the nobles knew, her husband included. She sat far enough away that none could imagine she heard every word. For an ordinary wife, this would be true, not so for Allyson, though she concealed her extra knowledge as much as possible. When her husband sat drinking with the scoundrel Hugh, it was best to know what passed between them.

"Pity one of us couldn't marry Isabella," Hugh muttered, tapping the painted ivory miniature of Princess Isabella of France that Randall held before him. "She's a pretty one, but I think the artist may've exaggerated her breasts, eh?" He tipped his head, considering that.

Randall had the good grace to flick an embarrassed glance at Allyson—as if he knew she could hear them--before replying, "It seems likely, but she's for the prince—Edward, that is, meaning no disrespect—"

Lord Hugh, Prince Hugh, Hugh the Bastard, depending upon whom one asked, waved this away, his gestures becoming more broad as the evening wore on, as they had each night since Edward II rode off without them. Allyson pricked her finger with her needle, scowled, and stuck the finger briefly between her lips to be sure she did not bleed upon Randall's new surcoat.

In the familiar hall of Carlisle Castle, attunement to her surroundings — the first step in any practice of her unusual skills — came easily. The room was not too large, with the thick walls necessary so close to the border, decorated with rather ordinary wall paintings and a few cheaply woven tapestries, a hearth to one side, a babble of footmen and knights at table between, and a handful of ladies like herself seated by the fire, including Hugh's own wife, Eleanor, who would likely be unsurprised by her husband's side of the conversation.

Distracted by the brief pain of the needlestick, Allyson extended her senses through her contact with the floor, her fine slippers barely impeding her, and focused on the head table, where her husband still sat, to the right of Hugh, who did not quite dare to occupy the center chair reserved for Prince Edward himself. Since his father's death a few weeks back, Edward was king in all but ceremony — well, that and demeanor. And the many other skills of kingship. That son had little of his father in him.

When the season for the Scottish campaign finished in rain, mud and defeat, as it always did, they would at last return to London for Edward II's coronation, and his father's funeral. In the meantime, the prince, after spending months cowering here in the castle in the name of grief, announced he would ride one last foray, in his father's honor — now, after the Scots had likely already retreated beyond a line of smoldering fields and ransacked granaries. Edward Longshanks, furious at the army's recent defeat, had vowed he should not be buried in state until Scotland was brought to heel. If he believed his feckless son would do the deed, the Longshanks would go to his grave a fool.

". . .two babes lost already, so I could hardly claim she's barren," Hugh said, now contemplating the portrait for himself. "You, on the other hand. . .you might easily put aside that spinster of yours and find something better." He wagged the picture of the French princess all the men had been mad for — all but Edward, whose tastes seemed to run in a different direction.

Allyson's teeth gritted together. Once more, Randall lifted his gaze toward her. Dark hair that hung to his shoulders framed his dark eyes and regular features, cheeks a bit too round, perhaps. The young lord was from an obscure family, smaller of stature than his more wealthy peers, but passably good-looking, everyone agreed, a good catch for a woman who'd lost one husband already. He came into the marriage eagerly enough, taking her with surprising restraint as she endured his attentions. She cried that first time, in spite of herself, and for his few visits after that kept her eyes squeezed shut. His attempts to romance her tapered off to none at all, maintaining the cold distance between them, thank God. She assumed he had already found a lover more receptive, and thanked that anonymous woman as well for deflecting her husband's lust.

Briefly, their eyes met, his face impassive. She dropped her gaze, scraping at the last stitch with her fingernail as if it was the stitching that annoyed her.

"What is it, are you taking her too rough?" Hugh asked, nudging Randall and grinning. "Babes won't grow if she doesn't enjoy it, or so my physician assures me."

Allyson listened closely, barely able to maintain the pretence of her stitchery.

"We've not been married very long, and her parents would be mightily put out if I set her aside." Picking at a plate of fruit on the table before him, Randall shrugged.

"But she never bore children for her first husband either—granted he only had her for a couple of years before his fatal fall." Hugh leaned back, spreading his hands. "You can't allow yourself to be bound to a woman who can't do what she's meant to. If Eleanor weren't pregnant again, I might well be thinking the same thing."

Randall frowned, his eyes deeper, as if he hadn't been thinking the same thing at all, and Allyson briefly wished she knew him better, to understand what currents flowed beneath those dark expressions. But in order to gain that knowledge, she'd have to suffer his touch. Better to remain aloof and ignorant.

"God grant this child is born healthy." Randall lifted his goblet.

"Hear, hear!" Hugh raised his goblet and drained it with a few swallows, then clunked it back on the table. "And a son. Who needs more women, eh?"

With a small, forced smile, Randall said, "It sounds rather cold when you put it that way, Hugh."

The bastard-prince snorted. With his flow of bright locks and vivid blue eyes, Hugh turned many a head, but "cold" barely touched upon the truth of the man. Even as little as she cared for her own husband, she could see that Randall possessed many qualities of honor and chivalry that Hugh either lacked or counterfeited.

Allyson still did not see how any friendship between the two survived.

"Well," said Hugh, "I do pay for masses to be sung for the babies, don't I? But I must be practical, especially given my. . .position." He raised his goblet toward the vacant chair of the absent king-to-be, whose heir Hugh remained until Edward saw fit to wed and bed the French princess. Lifting the goblet to his lips, Hugh frowned into its emptiness. "Wenches! Where's my wine?"

A girl hurried over, sloshing her jug as she went, only to earn another roar of his disapproval. Randall accepted a refill with a bit better grace, but she poured very little indeed, so he was not keeping up with his cousin's drinking. Good. The only thing Allyson enjoyed less than a husband's attention was that of a drunken husband.

"Pardon, m'lady," a young squire bowed before her, and Allyson acknowledged him.

"What is it, Silvio?"

His face looked terribly pale beneath a spray of freckles, his eyes very wide. "But you've pricked yourself, my lady," he said, impulsively taking her hand upon his, staring down at it, as if dazzled by the ring she wore. *I carry news from the river, my lady,* he told her, skin to skin, in the way of the magi, the witches as common folk would say.

Allyson's breath caught, for him to come to her in the hall, at such a time, was madness. News from the river? What were the magi speaking of tonight? *Tell me quick.*

Prince Edward — King Edward--is dead, fallen in a

skirmish with the Bruce.

Truly? There's no doubt?

He fell in the river, my lady. It was there that he died. Silvio's touch turned chill and she knew he did not merely carry the message, he had felt the prince's death stir the water, sweeping its truth downstream to any magus in contact with the water that night.

My God. Allyson sent him a sense of comfort and gratitude. Aloud, she said, "I'll be alright. What was it you came to tell me?" She polished a smile onto her face over the shock and dread that swirled through her.

"I. . . feel rather unwell," he blurted, drawing his chilled hands close and tucking them under his arms. "I beg leave to take my rest early. I can send one of the others—"

"Yes, of course," she told him. "Thank you for your service, Silvio. I'll be sure to inform my lord when he is at leisure."

Silvio bowed himself away from her, swaying slightly with an illness unfeigned. To lose Longshanks, and now his son! This was the most ill-omened campaign in the history of England to be sure. What would it mean for the rest of them? Allyson could barely breathe, but resisted the urge to cross herself: she alone in the hall knew of the death, and she could never tell how she had found out lest she and Silvio be known for witches. At the head table, Randall leaned close to listen to something Hugh was saying.

"You are too kind to them," Eleanor said, her French accented voice almost a purr. "You must learn to treat them firmly, as they need. Surely that boy's father did not squire him to your lord to be let off at the first sign of weakness?"

"I'm sure you're right, Lady Eleanor. But if my previous marriage and my own upbringing have shown me anything, it is that one gains more advantage in kindness than in cunning."

"How charming. Is that an aphorism of the north? Perhaps it explains how William was able to conquer your people so easily."

"Whereas the Welsh remain unconquered still," Allyson replied. "Even by you."

Eleanor darted a glance to her Welsh-raised husband and narrowed her eyes. "What do you mean by that?"

Sweetening her words with a smile, Allyson said, "Haven't you noticed? Both of our husbands have spent most of the evening in thrall to the portrait of that French princess—"then she broke off, bile suddenly rising in her throat. The French princess, promised to Edward, who now lay dead in a stream in Scotland. She pressed a hand to her mouth. "Come to that, my lady, I feel a bit unwell myself."

"You do look rather pale of a sudden." Eleanor shifted away from her, cupping one hand over her barely-rounded belly. "Do you suppose it was something you ate, you and that squire both? I sometimes imagine the cooks here are sympathetic with the Scots."

"You may be right about that," Allyson murmured, suddenly and painfully aware she might be addressing her future queen. "But have you been well? No more sickness?"

Eleanor smiled weakly. "None. I think the new physician is much better than the old one. Paris-educated, you know. The last one came out of Salerno, but I think their university is failing, like the rest of that mad nation."

The two women shared a chuckle as their moment of tension passed, Eleanor taking pride over her pregnancy, casting a pitying look to Allyson, who had yet to conceive even one child. Allyson accepted the pity, turning away. Physicians knew barely a whit about women, regardless of where they studied, compared to what a magus learned in her first months of awareness: how to stop her monthly courses, how to speak through the water, how to understand the presence of another, how to use contact and affinity to transform one thing into something else, how to encourage wounds to heal faster, how to listen from a distance. . . how to prevent a babe from taking root in a womb.

Randall looked a thousand miles away, just now, Hugh leaning one arm upon the empty chair, the chair that would remain empty — until he, himself would claim it. If he offered again, this time as king, for Randall to marry that French girl, would he do it? How would he not? He'd have to be a fool not to take such a boon, in service to a new king. Allyson's heart felt heavy and loud within her chest. It might be another day before the news reached them and Hugh realized what he could do. Longshanks had two other children by a French wife of his own, a woman who never matched his first wife for popularity. If she tried to seize the throne for one of her sons, England would become a French kingdom all over again, ruled by King Phillip of France on behalf of a boy-prince. Hugh, cold, calculating Hugh, might well be the better choice, and Randall would rise with him.

A clatter rose in the corridor outside, then the great

wooden door burst open and a lone knight stumbled in, breathing heavily. Allyson lurched to her feet. Already? Had the prince's sortie been so close by that a messenger could have come so quickly?

Then the newcomer raised his head, still panting, his dark hair hanging down around a small tonsure, his black and white tabard marked with the red cross of the Temple. His great stature alone should have given him away—Sir Robert! But he was in France.

A satchel thumping against his side, Robert stumbled up the rough aisle toward the head table, swinging his large head from one side to the next, gaping at the empty chair, his broad shoulders slumped in an instant. Her needlework quite forgotten, Allyson followed in his wake.

"Good Lord, Man, you might at least clean off the sweat before you burst in here!" Hugh shouted down at the knight, slapping the table.

At his side, Randall, too, rose up, forehead creased with worry. "I'm sure Sir Robert has good reason for his appearance."

Robert's head nodded, wagging a little too hard, and he swayed on his feet, clutching the shaft of the candelabra towering nearby. Unbidden, unnoticed, Allyson stepped up beside him, easing the heavy satchel from his shoulder to tuck under her arm. Then she slipped the goblet from Randall's place and held it out, whispering, "Robert."

With a nod, Robert put out his hand, dwarfing hers, and took the wine, swallowing a few draughts before Randall's face registered his startlement at the transfer of his own drink to his friend. His expression settled back to worry, but with a flicker of annoyance at his wife.

"I thank you, my lady," Robert breathed.

"So, what news could not bear keeping for even a hint of propriety?" Hugh's bright beard jutted as he scratched his chin.

"The French, my lords. King Phillip has badgered the Holy Father into defaming the knights—he's arresting every Templar in France. Seizing the property of the order. There's talk of torture, of," he gasped, took another swallow, and let the goblet slide back into Allyson's waiting hand, "of burnings for the unrepentant."

"Burnings! Now there's a show."

Randall's jaw took on that hard line Allyson so rarely saw, his eyes not leaving the knight's face. "King Edward has steadfastly refused to comply, Robert. The Templars of England have nothing to fear. I'm sure that Prince Edward will go forward with his father's wishes."

"His father's?" Robert cast about again, utterly at sea, and Allyson wanted to catch hold of his hand and find some way to reassure him. He had ridden hard, all across the land to reach Carlisle, not knowing until now that the king was dead.

"Edward Longshanks is gone," Hugh supplied. "My father passed away of an illness in July, God rest his soul." He fumbled his way through the sign of the cross, a gesture repeated by any within hearing. "Next time, God should take the Bruce instead—he was ill as well, but he seems to have recovered just fine."

Robert's face fell, his hair dangling in sweaty strands,

his own hand slowly and carefully forming the sign, his weariness grown deeper with every moment he stood. He needed more than wine and comfort, more than she could give—more than he would ever accept of her.

"As for Longshanks' heir, my brother, Edward II, has ridden off in one last raid before we take our father home to London to be buried. Randall and I are left as honor guard for the dead."

"This must be a second great blow to you, Robert." Randall gripped his friend's shoulder. "Let us find you some food and a place to sit."

Sliding back his hair with one hand, rubbing lightly over his tonsure, Robert sighed, "No, not until I've prayed for the king. But thank you. I'll be in the chapel." He gave a second bow, longer and more careful this time, flicked a smile at Allyson—a slight, bent smile—and took his leave, still impressive despite his disheveled state and the rumpled uniform of his order, the mark of his damnable calling.

"Arrested the knights and seized their lands. Holy Rood!" Randall slumped back into his chair, scrubbing his face with both hands.

"They are wealthy, and Phillip could use the funds," Hugh replied drily, then he glanced after Robert, eyes slightly narrowed, and it took no special skill to sense his calculations.

"My lord husband," Allyson blurted, then froze as both men stared at her from the advantage of their seats upon the platform, Hugh's gaze sharp, blue, dismissive, Randall's briefly warm, eternally worried. "I must speak with you, my lord."

"Women," muttered Hugh into his goblet, following

this with a snort of laughter.

"On what subject, my lady?" Randall addressed her politely enough. "You are welcome to speak with me at any time, of course," he added, attempting a smile. He smiled a lot when they first married, a bright-eyed expression that made him look more boyish than ever.

"It is not a matter I can speak of here, my lord." She ducked his gaze, her fingers knotting together, the needle stab oozing a drop of blood onto her surcoat. Privacy, even between man and wife, was a thing too little to be found in the over-stuffed castle.

At that, Hugh laughed uproariously. "The news from France has made her eager for you, my friend. And here I thought she might be frigid, but the idea of burnings seems to have lit a fire to her heart. You should seize the chance!" He smacked Randall on the arm.

"Thank you. By your leave, I think I will," Randall answered, shoving back his chair, offering a curt bow to the bastard prince. In three strides, he stomped down from the dais to stand before her, arms folded. "Where to, my lady? It seems I am yours to command."

Staring at Randall, his face closed and suddenly haughty, his arms crossed to keep her away, his jaw set against whatever she might say, Allyson swallowed hard and wanted to weep, to rant, to batter his chest with her weak fists. Anything to make him hear her. All these months she was relieved at the distance between them, and now that she needed him, she found him hard and distant as a saint carved upon a steeple. She might at least have been practical about the future and cultivated some sort of cordiality. "There's a chamber in the gatehouse, little used," she said. "My lord husband,"

and added a courtesy.

"Lead on, woman." He swept her ahead of him with one thrust of his arm.

Head bowed, flaxen braids sliding from beneath her veil, Allyson moved from the hall like a spirit, barely seen, but to be spoken of behind her back, the frigid wife of the popular lord, making him a spectacle before Hugh and all this company. Why not set her aside? Even granted her family's estates and connections, what good was a woman like her to a man like that? Her face glowed fiercely as the great door shut behind them. Randall spoke not a word, but his steps rap, rap, rapped after her down the stairs, between the tents of the knights and their entourages, out to the gatehouse. Overhead, clouds streaked the stars, obscuring in ragged wounds the lights of the heavens. The guards below let them pass up the stairs, to a narrow chamber alongside the watchmen's room. A table and a couple of benches stood to one side, while a tall bed filled the end of the room. Randall sat on the bed, pointedly so, his bearing angry, his expression so far from a seduction that Allyson might have laughed if she had no so felt like weeping.

She turned from him, setting down the satchel she'd taken from Robert to pick up one of the benches by an end to drag it closer. He half-rose as if to help her, but she dropped it into place before he could offer and settled onto it. Her fingers worked together again, like strands of silk too tangled to come free. Now that she had him here, she had no idea what to say, how to move him. Robert was his friend—many of the Templars were— surely he would need little convincing to convince

Hugh to make the right choices.

"What is it?" Randall demanded, and Allyson flinched, yanking her hands apart, sliding them into each opposite sleeve.

"I—forgive me, my lord husband. I shouldn't—I was too hasty, back in the hall."

"Hasty? Indeed, and bold as well, and now that I've come, you speak not a word to your intent. Christ on the Cross, woman, what do you want of me?"

Startled by his ferocity, Allyson found the tears beginning to spill. She forced them back, drew them back with all the strength of her will and of her magic. They were a woman's weapon, weak and foolish. She pressed her hands into her eyes as if thinking.

"Please, my lady." His voice came again, this time at a whisper. "I have seen you in all of your haughty grace, in all of your cold honor, I've seen you weep in the bed beneath me in spite of my care, and never have I seen you so distraught as now. Tell me what you will, my lady, I am listening."

Very slowly, Allyson lowered her hands and straightened her back, finding him leaning forward, elbows on knees, watching her intently, as no one had ever watched her before. "I must beg a boon of you, my lord. No more than I think that you would do in any case," she gave a nervous chuckle, "but you may not know the urgency of it."

"Very well," he said, shifting back again, still watchful, but more cautious. "What is your boon?"

"Mercy upon the Templars of England," she said.

The furrows returned to his brow, with a spark of incredulous laughter. "Mercy? On the Templars? Just who do you think you've married, my lady? I have no power over these things—you must ask it of Edward, though. . ."his dark glance slipped away, "I think he withholds from action against them less from mercy than from—"but he did not finish the sentence.

Cowardice? She wondered. Or fellow feeling? Some of the knights, like Prince Edward himself, were said to favor the company of men. But the prince was dead, and she had to persuade Randall without revealing that critical fact.

"I can't," she said, too quickly, drawing his eye, then hurried on to cover her mistake. "I'm only a woman, and he has little reason to listen to me. But you. . . you have influence. Hugh listens to you, surely, you can influence the prince—the princes," she stammered, then shook herself, beginning the magical process of attunement, struggling to find her balance again.

"Hugh listens to me—we're cousins, we were squires together for a time, before he went up to Longshanks' household, and it was he brought me into it, but I barely know Edward." He shrugged, letting his hands fall into his lap. "You interrupted us for this? To ask me for a thing I cannot give? Are you quite well, my lady?"

He tipped his head to study her, then his lips went still, a hard, straight line. "You're worried about him, aren't you. Months he's away, and you never even speak of him, then all he must do is ride in all covered with sweat, shaking with fear, and you leap to his defense. My God, do you think me blind?" Randall shoved to his feet, raking his hands through his hair, turning sharply from her, the solid strength of his back stiff as iron. Then, with a snarl, he slammed his booted foot into the bedstead.

Wood cracked. Allyson leapt up at the sound, knocking over her bench, nearly falling, but he had spun about to face her and caught her arm, pulling her back to her feet, staring into her face, breathing hard.

"Do you think me blind?" he repeated, soft and severe.

Allyson shook her head slightly, tears spilling over at last. The sense of his resentment flowed through their contact, rushing down her arm, making her tremble with the strength of the emotions he held back from her.

"He is your friend, too. I know it worries you."

"Worries me?" He shook her slightly, his eyes flared. "Indeed he is my friend, he has been, long before I knew what he meant to you."

And there it was, beneath his anger, beneath his hurt, the sharp, hot thrust of something else entirely. "There is nothing between us, my lord husband," she said, very carefully.

"I know it. For his sake, if not for yours. He takes his vows very seriously."

"He always has," she whispered.

"Has it always been so for you, even with your first husband, did Robert come between you?"

Allyson stood before him, ashamed. Her husband was no fool—how had she thought she was concealing her emotions? Her own mother, who taught her the ways of the magi, would be disappointed in her failure. But then her own mother had acquiesced to an arranged marriage for herself, then gave Allyson away first as a child, and again to the first man who came asking— though at least it took a long time in negotiation before her mother accepted Randall's suit.

She took a deep breath and gave him the truth. He deserved at least that.

"I was fourteen when my parents betrothed me to Henry," she murmured, then shook her head. "Henry was large, loud, brutish." Very nearly the opposite of level-headed, thoughtful Randall—worlds away from the chivalrous Sir Robert. She gave a shudder, wrapping her elbows in her hands, hugging herself, staring at the toes of her satin slippers where they peeked from beneath the hem of her gown. "I hated him, what he did, every time he touched me, every time he. . .took me. I don't know if you can, if a man could understand what it is to be a woman, a girl, really—"she gave a shake of her head, her braid tossing.

Randall's jaw took on that hard line. "It must have been awful for you."

"One night," another deep breath, and she lifted her chin to meet her husband's gaze, "I decided to run away from Henry. Robert was a young squire, then. I barely knew him, or any of the other men of the household. I couldn't go on foot, not far, so I fled to the stables, and I saw Robert there, tending the horses. I asked him in the name of Holy Mary to help me escape. He didn't ask what my trouble was, he didn't argue with me or try to hold me, he just saddled me a horse." Tears streaked her face again as she looked into the past, and she flicked them away with her fingers. "His own horse, I think— he's too honest a man to steal, even on behalf of a lady. So I rode out, but I had barely gotten to the moat that surrounded our manor before Henry called after me, drunk, furious. I could hear him shouting at me from the rampart, and then. . . I heard him fall."

She wet her lips, but Randall said nothing, his hands lightly held, head cocked, regarding her with absolute absorption. "I turned back immediately. I hated him, but I didn't want him to be hurt."

"His neck was broken," Randall supplied. "I had taken on the management of a manor nearby, I used to pay calls at Henry's all the time. I heard about his death, that he'd gotten drunk and staggered out on the ramparts. Not the rest." He nodded slightly. "Robert rescued you. Of course you care for him."

Sniffling, wiping her eyes, Allyson nodded miserably. "I went back to my family and barely saw him. He was elevated to knighthood a year or two later, and joined the Temple almost immediately."

"I wish I had known." Randall traced a scar on the back of his hand.

"You wouldn't have married me," she supplied.

With a violent slash of his hand, Randall said, "Don't be a fool, woman. If I had known Henry was hurting you, I should have insisted on the king's intervention." For a moment, he stared at her, breathless, his dark gaze shifting over her face, his hand falling into a fist.

Then his hands spread, the slightest grim smile returning to his lips. "It is ridiculous, my lady wife, that our first real conversation should begin with you beseeching my aid for the man that you love." His voice fell upon her, rough and rigid as the bedboard he had cracked with his anger, and she flinched, expecting at any moment that anger to be turned fully upon herself.

She bowed her head, her cheeks flaming, the heat battling with the cold of her heart and of her trembling hands.

"I will help Robert, of course—I'll do what I can for any member of the order, but really, I have no power here. I am a lesser son, my lady; it's only the lands you brought to the marriage that give me any standing at all, that and Hugh's friendship."

Hugh's friendship gave him more power than he knew, and Allyson struggled with her secret knowledge. Randall believed she asked him only because of her feelings for Robert—even if he had seen that calculating look on the future king's face, he would not know how close indeed that danger lay. Hugh would need money to consolidate his power if he would claim the throne, money to hold off the Scots, to rebuild the border, to woo the barons' support. Robert and his order represented a harvest of lands and gold that a man like Hugh could only dream of.

"I've not made a great effort to cultivate Prince Edward's favor—not in that way," he added drily—"but I could do so. You've gone gray again. I did say I didn't want that sort of favor from the prince," he said, with a touch of that humor she recalled from the early days of their union. "I believe what I told to Robert, that Edward II will uphold his father's defense of the Templars. You ask what is not needed, from a man who cannot provide it."

And on behalf of a man who would not approve her involvement. Allyson searched for a way to overcome Randall's resistance, to convince him of the urgency of her request, now, before word spread and he became so embroiled in Hugh's scheming that he might go along with the bastard's wishes, even to the detriment of the

Templars. She had no sway over him, and knew of only one course that might show the need. "Something has happened, something known by only a few—a thing that will change our realm forever." She swallowed. "Please believe me, my lord husband, Edward is dead."

He nodded slightly. "In July."

She put our her hands to stop him. "Prince Edward, Edward the Second of England. He fell in a skirmish with the Scots."

"What?" He bolted to his feet, catching her shoulders. "But that's--How have you heard this, and we have not?" Then his eyes flared. "That boy, who came to you in the hall, he told you, didn't he? He should have announced it to all, or you should have. What's the meaning of this?"

And with his words went any hope of concealing Silvio's involvement. All this time she thought her husband barely noticed her when he wasn't trying to get a child, and now, to find he'd been watching her— it made her nervous, self-conscious in a way she had not been before. "I cannot tell you how he knew, just as he could not tell Prince Hugh. Let us say he is. . . a visionary, but one whose visions so often come true that I have learned to heed them. He tells me that Edward fell in battle with the Scots, that he fell into the river, more than a day's ride hence. The news will come, my lord husband, you must believe me."

"Until lately," Randall answered, "I have had little reason to doubt you." His hands slid from her shoulders, folding across his chest, his boot heel nudging the broken board. "What might a woman say on behalf of her leman?"

"He isn't!" she shot back, "and you know it—you've just said so yourself, that he would never--!"

"But in your heart you wish he were. By God, lady, it is your heart that makes it so. I thought I knew you, even to suspecting this—"he waved his hand at her and Robert's satchel, brought here by her own hands—"but how can I know what lies you might invent? You would not deign to use a woman's wiles upon me, not even in our own bed chamber, you would not use them now. What else is left to you, but such an outrageous lie? And what do you think I can do with it? Extract a promise from Hugh to leave the Templars and their lands alone?"

Allyson's heart thudded with the realization that she might well be pushing him further away, further toward Hugh and the French Princess, further even from Robert who had for so long been his friend. In trying to aid the knight, she might well be the cause of his destruction. She sank onto the bench once more, shaking, almost wishing she could touch him, use her magic to influence him, but to reach for him now, after his accusations, would only paint her all the more an adulterer if only in her heart.

"You may freely call me liar and believe it so—in time you'll hear the truth and then believe it." A tear slipped down her cheek but she forced herself to face him, to imagine what he might say. "I care not for myself, my lord husband, but imagine what would be if what I say is true. Prince Hugh would claim the crown at Edward's death, would he not? And then? The Bruce returned from his illness stronger than ever—slaying the heir of Longshanks will make him stronger still, even if he cannot face our entire army. If Hugh must race to London to seize his power, he cannot afford to leave the border as it stands. He will need armies. The Holy Father has already given his blessing to the seizure of Templar lands. Do you think that Hugh would let them be? You, my lord, know him better than any man. Ask not what I am capable of—I'm only a woman—but Prince Hugh—what might he do to secure the crown?"

She wet her lips, gazing up at him, a towering figure, once more the distant saint, but this time, listening, scowling, to her plaint. "Believe me a liar, believe me faithless, feckless and cold, my lord husband, but do not let your feelings about me obscure your judgment. You have many friends among the Templars, and they will need a voice at the new king's ear."

Randall's dark hair swung forward, shadowing his face. "You keep more faith with me than I believed, lady, if you think my voice could have such power."

"I do," she breathed. "I do believe it." She did not have to like the man to know his strengths; talking sense was, indeed, among them.

He straightened and spread his hands at last. "Best sleep with the ladies tonight. I have not the heart to have you close." So saying, he turned and strode away, his boots rapping down the stairs as he left her behind.

Would he speak out for the Templars? She did not know, but she did not think he was the sort of man to allow Robert and his companions to be tortured or burned for jealousy. Her eyes fell to the cracked board, broken by his fury when she admitted her love for Robert. What made him most furious, that he was nearly cuckolded by his wife, or that it should be his own dear friend she loved? Perhaps she did not know

Randall even as well as she believed. Robert, too, must be warned of what was coming.

She pushed off from the bench, took up the heavy satchel, its weight bearing down her arms as if it carried so much more than a knight's travelling things, and walked down more slowly in her husband's wake. Sleep with the ladies. Not an unfamiliar state, but one that often marked those ladies whose husbands' beds were warmed by someone else—another humiliation atop her hastily dragging him from the hall. Hugh and the rest of the men would cheer Randall's forsaking her. She thought again of the French princess, now lacking a betrothed, and wondered if Randall had thought of her as well. He could give up Allyson's lands and titles in exchange for something better, even did it not involve a comely new wife, perhaps more willing than the first. Politics, not personal. Randall had little personal investment in her as a wife, merely in the prestige she brought him.

The chapel stood aside by the kitchens and joined with them along a passage to the keep where Randall likely returned to take his wine and the rowdy suggestions of his comrades as to what he and his wife had been doing in their absence and why he returned alone. When she found the chapel door standing open, a few candles lit around the altar, Robert was already rising, crossing himself, his back to the door, swaying with exhaustion, setting a hand upon the wall of the narrow room, and giving a sad shake of his head.

"Robert? Are you finished at prayer?"

Straightening, Robert tugged down and smoothed out his tabard, then slowly came to the door, ducking his head a little to emerge into the corridor before her. "Aye, lady. There shall be more later, no doubt, but I pray that God and Longshanks both will forgive a man his hunger."

At the word, at the sight of him, and the scent of sweat and leather, Allyson's belly tightened. Hunger, indeed, but she knew full well that was not the sort of hunger he meant. "I've brought your things. The kitchen is just along here." She nodded in that direction, and took it as a mark of his exhaustion that he did not try to take the satchel, but merely drifted along to the kitchen where a bright fire still danced around great pots of stew and pottage, round loaves laid out along a counter, the snoring forms of a few scullions taking up one corner. She pushed aside a stack of trenchers and a jug of mead to set down the satchel on a broad table. "Sit, please, Robert. Let me serve you."

"'Tis no task for a lady," he sighed, and then bowed his head. "But I submit this once." Sinking onto a stool, he dragged his satchel closer, placing his hands upon it as on something holy, his attention absorbed by some deeper matter.

Silently, Allyson took up a drinking bowl and filled it with mead to place at his elbow, then filled one of the trenchers with bread, stewed beef and roasted onions, cinnamon duck, and a mound of the baked apples he loved so well. She slid this before him as she took a stool opposite. "Eat up, Robert. You'll need your strength."

That brought his eyes up, startled, and he said, "Indeed, my lady, and you don't even know the extent of that." He hooked the trencher with one finger, dragging it to the other side, then flipped open the leather satchel and removed an object wrapped in linen. Unwinding this revealed a cup that glinted in the firelight.

"Oh, you wish to use your own! I should have asked. Here, let me fill it." She reached out, but Robert jerked the cup away.

"Saints preserve us, lady, no!" He stared down at the cup in his hand, a modest-sized vessel, even given the size of those hands, but, now that it was turned to the light, it shone with gold and glittered with a rim of gems. "I'm not fit to drink from this one. I don't know that any man under the heavens would be."

Robert was fit for any finery as far as Allyson believed, but his humility was among his more attractive virtues. The reverence in his voice brought her around the table beside him, shoulder to shoulder as she stood gazing at the golden cup, a thing of wealth and beauty, the treasure of some monastery perhaps, or a ritual vessel for the Templars themselves.

"What do you make of it?" he breathed, still speaking as if at church on Easter Sunday.

"It's beautiful," she said. "May I?" she held out a hand, and he studied her face before he handed over the cup.

Allyson gasped, nearly dropping it as a shock of cold and wonder thrilled through her palm. Robert's arm wrapped her shoulders, his other hand supporting hers beneath the cup. "My lady, are you well?" he asked, but his eyes lit with excitement, their weariness receding. "It is, isn't it? You feel it, too."

Too? She wanted to ask. Robert was no witch, not like her or Silvio, but neither was she especially sensitive, even for her kind, and yet, she had felt the presence of this object, a brooding, powerful thing, a talisman with layers of emotion, almost as complex as a man. "What is it?" she murmured, suddenly understanding his reverence.

Too soon he withdrew the warmth of his arm and slid the cup from her nerveless palm. "The Grand Master sent it with me, to get it out of France. He thought it would be safe here. Now, I am not so sure." Once more, he held the cup in the firelight, tilting it so that the gems caught the light, and the dark interior filled with darkness. His throat worked with emotion, and she did not need to touch him to sense the stirring of something close to tears as he told her, "It is the cup of our Lord Jesus Christ, the cup that gathered his blood as He died upon the Cross." He drew a deep and trembling breath. "It's the Grail."

RANDALL LAY in the guest quarters in a bed too large for only one, pretending to snore. It seemed hardly worth the effort—Hugh's own snores covered any other sound except the rhythmic rapping of a bed at the other side occupied by one of the other lords and a wench from the town below the castle. The sound made him clench his jaw, Allyson's face lingering before him, lovely, pale and closed as ever. She'd likely gone straight to Robert, using the excuse of his baggage to bring her to his side—and Randall had driven her there. Idiot. Robert and Allyson had never consummated the love she bore him, that much was plain, even if Robert's vows held him back, but now that the Templars were officially disbanded, how much longer would he cling to the order, especially when presented with a woman who loved him?

Randall rolled over sharply, yanking up the blankets around his shoulder. Robert would rather die than betray a friend. But if she offered the love she denied to her husband, what then? Randall mistrusted celibacy, at least as a choice. What man could truly abandon carnal desire, and even the most holy of men must, at least some time, be tempted. Allyson was barely nineteen, beautiful, and her very aloofness could be a lure to a certain sort of man—the sort who would love to see her chilly surface broken by passion. God!

Shoving the blankets back, Randall sat up, pressing his bare feet to the floor, shoulders slumped. If he told her the truth, the real reason he married her, would she bend? Times he felt she must already know, and simply didn't care, then times like that evening—was she so cruel as to say those things, to beseech him like that if she had known? He scrubbed his hands over his face and pinned back his hair, gripping his skull in both hands. If she were a liar—as yet there had been no word of Edward II's death--then so was he. Tell her. Find her now, tell her now, abase himself, embarrass himself again as she had embarrassed him before all that company. Either that or wring her lovely neck.

The image before his eyes shifted to skin more pale, hair black and lustrous, a bosom swelling an embroidered gown: Isabella, princess of France, legendary beauty. Hugh had said in his cups that Randall should give over Allyson and marry Isabella, but Randall knew it for a jest. Absent Allyson's lands, he himself had little but the favor of the bastard prince. If, on the other hand, the bastard prince became a second bastard king. . . Randall groaned. Allyson had no wish to be married with him in any case. So. Let her go.

Or tell her the truth.

Pushing himself up, Randall found his hose and pulled them on, securing his belt beneath his woolen tunic, Allyson's embroidery smoothing over his thighs. She made such an excellent counterfeit of marriage. He found his boots beneath the low bed and tugged them on, then stepped over and around the sleeping knights and squires and headed for the next floor, where the ladies kept their bower.

A sleepy maidservant startled awake at his approach, scrambling up from her blankets. "Yes, my lord?"

"I'm looking for my wife," he told her, and the momentary gleam of hope in her eyes dimmed as she gave him a courtesy. The maids on duty here must expect the advances of those menfolk who prowled the night—might count on it, in fact, which might explain the maid's low, tight bodice and skirt hitched up to reveal her ankles.

"Yes, my lord, but the Lady Allyson's not here, my lord." Another courtesy, this time with bowed head.

Randall growled, and the maid withdrew a little into herself, hands knotting in her skirt. "Any idea where she might be?"

"No, my lord."

"Thanks." He turned from her, stalking down the corridor, tempted to thunder round the spiraled stair, but forcing himself to patience. All resolve to speak to Allyson faded with the growing conviction that he had been right. It was not the company of ladies she'd been seeking.

Men-at-arms and servants cluttered the floor and benches of the hall, some still awake to roll dice or stoke the great fire in the hearth. A few of these bobbed their heads, alert and ready to respond to his command, but happy enough to subside to their places at a wave of his hand. For a moment, Randall wished his parents were still alive to be feted at their youngest son's invitation, here, at the left hand of kings, to see him obeyed, desired, listened to—and maybe cuckolded by the wife he had insisted on securing. His fists clenched and he walked faster, pushing through a smaller door into the corridor beyond. The chapel door stood open, nubs of candles burnt to almost nothing at the altar and Robert long departed.

As he stood, staring, thinking what to do, a rumble of voices reached him from the kitchens. He stalked inside, the servants' murmur ceasing abruptly as they rose to bow to him. "What's yer pleasure, laird?" said one of them, his words a mouthful of nearly-Scottish dialect.

"I'm looking for my wife—tall lady, clad in blue with a silver fillet in her hair, braids down her back." His hand moved over his head and down, describing her.

"We 'ad one like that, aye, laird, but she's off now."

"Clearly," Randall snarled, "but where?"

The two servants exchanged a glance, and the fellow shrugged. "Dunno, m'laird, but not 'ere, any road."

"Fine, then. How about a very tall knight, wearing the cross of the Templars?"

The fellow flicked a glance at his companion, but that layabout cut his eyes swiftly toward the dim recesses where another door stood in the shadows. "Not 'ere either, m'laird," said the spokesman.

Randall planted his fists at his hips. "Let me guess. Both were here, both are gone, and they left this place together."

"In a manner o' speaking, laird, but I said nothing 'bout it, did I?" The lout busied himself picking at a stain on his apron.

"And you?" Randall pounced on the other man. "What did you see?"

"Nothing, laird. I've been sleeping, 'til just now when this cur woke me." He offered a scowl to his companion, his grubby face creasing, one fist waving as if to cuff him, a ring winking in the dim light.

"Did they swear you to secrecy? Toss you a coin, is that it?"

"No, laird, course not," the first man replied. "It was their going that woke me is all, and I hate to be the one to give bad news, 'specially to the likes of you, eh?" He tried a grin, revealing a mouthful of crooked teeth with a couple of gaps.

"Thank you," Randall snapped, clamping his jaw shut before he laid into the scullion as he so longed to. Pounding by, he pushed through to the hall and found the spiral stair that would take him back to bed. On the verge of the broad guest chamber, though, Randall hesitated. The anger that surged through him would not allow for sleep and his jaw already throbbed from the clenching of his teeth. Where would they go? How had they imagined they might keep such a tryst secret?

It was madness. Taking a lantern from its shelf by the door, he worked his way across the thicket of sleeping servants, peering at one face, then another, until he recognized young Silvio, the squire who had spoken to Allyson after supper.

Before he could nudge the youth awake, Silvio's eyes snapped open, flaring white in the glow of the lantern.

"Get up," Randall said, moving swiftly back to give the squire room.

With a hurried fetching of shoes and fumbling of clothes, the boy followed him, hopping on one foot as he shod the other, then tugged at his tabard and gave a sloppy bow. He met Randall's gaze, his brows pinching together, eyes ringed.

"The Lady Allyson. Where is she?"

"D—I'm—I don't know, my lord," the youth stammered, then he gave a toss of his head like a nervous colt, shifting toward the stairs, eyes twitching.

"What is it, boy? You're anxious as a virgin bride." Poor choice of words, Randall thought, wincing to himself, but Silvio flinched, his fingers clenching and releasing.

"I don't know, my lord, that is, I thought she was downstairs."

"In the ladies' quarters."

A hesitation. "My lord—"

"Don't bother lying," Randall ground out. He grabbed the boy's shoulder, eliciting a soft yelp, and propelled him in front down the stairs. Silvio stumbled ahead into the darkness, his hand trailing the wall, nearly falling the whole way as he went so that Randall regretted his harshness—but surely he had not pushed him so roughly as that.

The squire continued, off-balance, back down to the hall, but staggered free of the stairs in the direction of the kitchen, not the hall, and froze, arms slightly spread, knees flexed. Allyson had said the boy was a visionary, and now, seeing him like this, Randall could well believe it. He'd had few signs of the boy's fey nature during his few months tenure at their estate so far, but this behavior was bizarre—even granted he'd woken the boy from a sound sleep and startled him with questions.

"So. You expected her to be in the kitchen? Him, too? You knew they were together?" Randall knotted his fist in the boy's tunic and dragged him along, but Silvio kept his balance this time, almost dragging Randall in turn, as if eager to get there.

"My lord," he blurted, "yes! I mean, no. They were here, yes, but not together, not—"he flung up his hands in frustration. "Holy Mary, my lord, I'm making a mess of things."

"I'd say so." Randall released him with a final nudge so that the boy's quick steps carried him straight to the large table at the center of the room. He fetched up against it with both hands, gasped as if he'd been struck a body blow. At that, Randall stepped back from him, circling round until he faced the lad across the table, holding up the lantern to get a look at his face. Silvio's parents were distant relations of Allyson's, which was why they sent him to Randall for his knightly training, but even on the practice field, he'd never shown himself so sensitive to the slightest force. Mayhap it was the touch alone that did it.

Whatever might be the matter, now they'd come this

far, Silvio glanced around distractedly, not even looking at his sworn lord. The scullions had gone, leaving the place empty but for their scattered blankets by the door. No, those were sacks of some kind. The scullions seemed to have rolled up their blankets and taken them along.

Slamming the lantern down on the table, Randall propped open its translucent horn door to allow the candle inside to shed more light. This made Silvio's cheekbones shadow his eyes, but could not conceal their anxious darting as he prowled around the side of the table, one hand sliding over its surface.

"Tell me straight, Silvio, and tell me the truth before I take it from your hide. Where is my wife?"

The squire faced him, his mouth drawn, his expression stricken. "In faith, my lord, I do not know. Last I knew of her, she was here, fetching mead for Sir Robert." His hand spread upon the surface, pressing into it.

"You saw them together."

"No, my lord." Silvio shook his head, his curls bouncing. "Forgive me, my lord, I must seem mad to you, but please—" He shook his head again, glancing around, looking down, his eyes glossy as if with tears, his throat working.

"By God, why has everyone around me got to weeping? Have I given you any cause to fear me?" Randall swept his arms open, the lantern flame flickering at the motion.

"No, my lord, not you." Still, he trembled.

Something in the boy's demeanor pierced Randall's anger and he reached out, gently and steadily to place his hand on the boy's shoulder. "Silvio, forgive me my anger. It is not you I'm angry at," he said, softly but firmly. "Not I, you said, and yet clearly you are afraid. Tell me why."

"For her," Silvio breathed, almost leaning into Randall's hand. "There has been violence here, my lord. They left together, 'tis true enough, but not alone—and not by their own will." His eyes squeezed shut, his off-hand propping up his forehead.

"Violence?"

Silvio made no reply, his breathing shaky, and Randall guided him to a high stool and pressed him to sit. A visionary. Well, then. Randall took up his lantern again, and tossed a few more logs on the fire, sending up a spray of sparks.

The place smelled of stews and mead, and Randall's boots stuck to the floor by the table, then one of them struck something that skittered further beneath the table. Bending down, Randall caught sight of an object rocking gently there: a shard of pottery with the broad sweep of a rounded jug. In this low light, it looked as if a jug had spilled upon the floor, making a sticky splatter toward the roasting pit, but this one piece, tucked beneath the table was the only shard. Evidence of something, but likely only of a scullion's carelessness. Mayhap that's why they'd left. But then, if the jug were spilled so recently, the floor would be damp, not sticky. No, this mess had been made and the shards removed hours ago. Perhaps while his wife served mead to Sir Robert.

Randall straightened slowly, frowning. None of this made any sense whatsoever. The idea of his wife running off into the night with the man she loved—that made a story he could believe, assuming he believed Robert would betray him. Robert and Allyson both taken under duress? Preposterous. For one thing, Robert was a Templar knight, a formidable opponent, even without his weapons, and fairly taller than any man in the royal party, saving only Edward Longshanks himself, God rest him.

"I can't find her, not from here," Silvio murmured, head bowed into his hands.

Robert may not have imagined it as a tryst. Allyson might have persuaded him to some more innocent adventure, with this boy set to cover their trail by whatever web of lies he cared to manufacture. Except he had been asleep in the chamber by the time Randall had arrive there and, in his angry, wakeful state, Randall would have noted any other comings and goings. Silvio had spoken to no one until Randall woke him up.

"Tell me what you know," Randall commanded.

"But my lord, I cannot say how I know it," the boy replied. He gazed up at Randall now with genuine pleading, with that anguished look of a dog who knows it has failed its master.

"I do not care how you know it, boy. Tell me now."

Silvio nodded vaguely and pushed himself up. "They sat here—Sir Robert here, anyhow. She stood by him, then—there's fear, my lord. It's not. . .not a thing I see." He rubbed his fingers together as if feeling for the right words, then prowled past Randall who turned to track him with his eyes. "I—there's so little." He stood facing the far door, then raised his hand to the doorframe with a cry so sharp, Randall thought he'd jerk back a hand with a bleeding gash.

Jogging the few steps over, raising the lantern high, Randall saw what had turned the boy's skin to ash. A smear of blood marked the lintel, with a few strands of Robert's dark hair. A man too tall, forced out the door. A difficult foe to overcome, unless it were Allyson who was first attacked — and Robert, sworn defender, who dare not risk her life in combat. Or a man so eager to flee with his companion that he knocked his own traitorous head upon the lintel.

Randall yanked the door open. It lead into the yard, not unexpectedly, alongside the tower with the royal apartments. To one side stood the postern gate, a narrow door that lead outside the walls. Randall stalked closer, his lantern providing a swaying pool of light, Silvio stumbling after. The postern gate stood closed, but unbarred, as if someone had let themselves out without leaving anyone behind to reseal the entrance. This door, too, he pulled open, staring down the hill toward the moat drawn from the river beyond. If Allyson lured Robert out here for a tryst, they could not pass the moat, but there was plenty of thick grass around the castle walls on the slope leading down to the water. Randall prowled first one way, then the other, lantern high, listening for his wife's voice, for her laughter, until his boot toes nudged the moat itself, lapping at his feet.

His boots were not the only ones to tramp this bank tonight: others crushed the grass and scuffed the mud about, and a cleft in the bank showed where a boat had been brought up. He could not quite see to the other side. A boat? Allyson had not even known Robert would be in England — she could not have planned for this.

"Who goes?" called a voice from above, accompanied

by a clatter of arms.

"Lord Randall Grimbaud and my squire—we found the postern gate unbarred. I think the scullions have been trysting by the moat. No sign of them now. You haven't seen anything, have you?"

The guard leaned down. "Was some peasants with a cart on the other side, my lord, a few hours back. Seemed to have overshot the bridge. I sent 'em back the right way."

"I see. Well, we'll lock up on our way in."

"Much obliged, my lord! Fare you well."

Randall raised a hand as they turned back for the keep. Before he'd even slid the bar home, Silvio was dancing around before him, hands clasped. "A boat, my lord, and a cart—at night? Something awful's happened, I know it."

With a swift, solid pressure, Randall pinned the boy against the wall of the passage with his forearm, the lantern gripped tight and his bootknife already in his other hand, its tip angled at Silvio's throat. "More awful than the death of kings?"

The squire's face drained of color, his lips parted. "She told you," he breathed, forgetting Randall's title completely.

The boy's expression erased any doubts Randall still had about whether young Edward still lived. "How did you know about Edward II?"

Head tipped to the side, Silvio did not answer.

"Are you working for the Bruce?"

"No, my lord!" That brought a flame into his cheeks, but had he answered so quickly because it was true? If the boy were a traitor, then so was Allyson—and this entire night staged for reasons known only to the Scots. The only reason she revealed her knowledge, and confirmed her source, was to save Robert from a danger only she perceived. The boat, the cart might have been part of some other plan entirely, a plan which Robert's appearance jeopardized when it compromised Allyson herself.

"Saddle two horses and meet me by the main gate. Be prompt, or I'll not wait for the king to give you justice."

"I am no traitor, my lord, I swear it! Nor is she."

"And yet you've both woven round me a web of lies and omissions. What you are, I do not know, but I will before this night is out, Silvio, and it's only your parents' honor and hers that keeps me from rousing the entire keep to go after them."

He retreated a step, releasing Silvio who sketched a bow and ran for the stables. The knife returned to its sheath and Randall hurried to the armory to reclaim his other weapons, a travelling cloak, a sword for Silvio—if he determined the boy could be trusted. A cart could not travel fast, not as fast as men on horseback to be sure, but the traitors knew the territory while Randall must find his way in the dark. No longer certain if he tracked a wayward wife, a victim or a spy, Randall girded himself for battle, to meet whatever might come.

ALLYSON CEASED struggling against the dirty wool that covered her face and lay still, as still as could be, bouncing in the cart over rough terrain. Trouble was, when she tried to begin the process of attunement, gathering her magical senses to understand where they was and what was happening to them, she heard over and over again Robert's grunt of pain after the solid sound of bone on wood. He had dodged the blanket that should have swaddled him — that much she saw before she'd been taken up by their assailants. Something shattered and thick voices ordered Robert's compliance. They did not need to voice the threat — she felt it jabbing at her own spine: if he disobeyed them, they would kill her.

"Wha'd ya do that for? Tha's not what we were set to do," someone muttered. "Take the prince's brother, aye, take a knight who might be privy to the plans, aye, but this? This is madness."

"Never you mind — you just keep on as you've done."

"Oh, aye, but it's all down to you when the bishop finds out. Just doing as you say, myself," muttered the first man, younger, Allyson reckoned, with a less cultured accent.

"Shut up, the both of you — or give a hand with the cart if you've got so much spirit," grunted a voice from behind.

The cart gave a sudden lurch and pitched to the side. Allyson threw her weight against it, toppling the whole thing to the ground and rolling free of her blanket.

"Damn all — catch the bag!" The older man glared at Allyson as he plunged by her on the treacherous slope, slithering down and crowing when he snatched Robert's satchel.

"You've got what you want," she said aloud. "Leave us right here." She took two quick steps forward to the shadow of the cart where Robert lay sprawled, blinking, his mouth gagged with a strap, hands bound with another one. In the dim light, she saw a bloody scrape at his temple, but couldn't tell how bad it was.

The fellow's eyes twitched from one of them to the other, then he said, "Can't do it. Get him up. Get back in the cart."

"No good, Archie, the wheel's broke," complained the younger voice, a scullion she recognized from serving at table earlier. He ducked her glance.

The third man, broad-shouldered and still clad in a cook's apron spread his hands. "He's right about that, Archie, and ye should at least be telling us what you've got on, since—"but he broke off at Archie's hiss, and tip of the head toward Allyson.

Each of the three men carried a long knife, and the cook had a cleaver tucked in his belt. Ahead of them, returning now as the growing strength of the light indicated, walked a fourth man clad in leather and bearing an ax. This man held up his torch to survey the scene and gave a growl. "Fine. Off the road." He glanced around and pointed the torch toward the wooded slope above. "Up there. Donald and Lachlan'll be along with the others, then we head overland. We're too close to Carlisle."

Others. Allyson's throat felt dry, and not just from breathing in the wool. She knelt at Robert's side, touching his shoulder, the sense of his strength, his worry, his courage flowing to her through the contact. His pain was slight, deliberately exaggerated for the sake of their guards, and Allyson suppressed her smile, stroking her fingers along the edge of the wound. "He's injured. He can't travel like this."

"He'll have to," snapped the newcomer, swinging out his ax toward Robert's exposed throat. "Or I can leave him right here."

"No!" Allyson cried, throwing herself forward.

"Ivor, don't," Archie protested, clutching the satchel. "Don't. Still too close, as you said. A broken cart, anybody might leave, but a puddle of blood? That's another problem."

Ivor straightened, but still gripped the ax. "So get him up, Archie. It's your stage now you've gone against orders, but I'm warning you, Archie, there's only so much the rest of us'll do on your say-so."

This suggestion of restraint carried a twinge of irony. Ivor would willingly murder an English knight in the street on his own authority — what would he deny to Archie's?

"C'mon, on your feet, or off wi' your head." Archie grinned as he spoke, but his eyes looked pinched, and Allyson could sense his urgency. He was keen to do whatever he had in mind, but keen, too, that Robert should live to be there.

"Perhaps, of their mercy, they'll allow me to see to your wound when we stop for rest," Allyson said. "In the meantime, you must lean on me."

Robert's eyes flared, just a little, and he gave a muffled groan as she helped him roll to his feet, trying to steady him as he pitched and staggered, letting his head hang down, hair over his face. Allyson pressed herself to his side, giving the appearance of support, giving a prayer of thanks as he leaned, just a little, on her, the heat of his presence filling her, her magical senses yearning toward him. She tried to ignore the strains of honor and the much more devout prayer she sensed that ran beneath his skin. They were a part of him, as she wished that she could be.

Four men—how many could Robert handle, presuming they could gain a knife from one of their assailants? She hoped for a moment of privacy, perhaps while she tended his injury, during which she could whisper a plan. She wished, too, that she were brave enough to share the truth of what she was, what she could do, but it was there that all her hopes failed. She could convey her thoughts to him through his skin, without speaking at all, but he would know her for a witch. No knight sworn to the Cross could suffer a witch to live.

Pushing beneath a few low-hanging bows, they came to the top of the rise, a grassy dell made dark with shadows. Just at the edge of the torchlight, three standing stones thrust up from the grass, tipped slightly, sentinels of the ancients. Ivor finally put away his ax as Allyson let Robert down to kneel on the ground, then the Scotsman gripped Robert's chin, holding up the torch to see him better.

"Barely a scratch." He released his hold on the prisoner. "And I know for a fact you English have heads hard as rock, specially when it comes to other men's rights." Withdrawing, Ivor spat a gobbet that landed on Robert's mud-streaked tabard. Tension shot through him, but Allyson kept her soothing hands upon him. Now was not the time to answer insult.

"What do you want of us?" Allyson demanded.

"Yes, Archie, what?" Ivor turned on his heel, both

of them staring at Archie who perched on a log a little way off, turning out Robert's possessions—ink and parchment scraps, spoons, shaving kit, various leather-wrapped parcels tumbling to the grass--until he thrust in his hand and gave a sigh, his face alight, and leaned over the satchel, looking inside.

Ivor and the cook drew closer, while the young man blurted, "How can you be sure it's the Grail?"

Holding the torch over their heads, Ivor stared down and the big man crossed himself. "It's what we need him for," Archie said, with a tip of his head toward the prisoners. "He's a Templar, see, one of the guardians. We need to show we got it from him."

As their guards had moved away, Allyson was already sliding her hands along Robert's bonds, pretending to untie the strap at his wrists while she called upon her skill, using the talisman she kept at her breast to strengthen the magic and a bit of thread loose at her own wrist to create the affinity between thread and strap so that she could cause the knot to loosen itself. She did not remove the strap completely, but left it loose, his wrists sliding free whenever he wished. He seized her fingertips and gave a gentle squeeze.

"So that's why you broke with orders and nabbed these two. Even if it's not what you say, we're rich," Ivor crowed, his grin revealing jagged teeth.

"Nothing like that," Archie shot back, slapping down the flap of the satchel. "It's for the Bruce."

"Bruce don't need it more'n we do, Archie," Ivor said. "These English'll be off before autumn's truly set in, and more folk're flocking to him all the time. One more victory and we'll be marching on the English next summer." He turned his grin on Allyson and Robert.

Allyson's stomach felt hollow. One more victory—
and they did not know they had it already. With the
death of Edward Longshanks already demoralizing
the soldiers, the death of his son might well dissolve
the whole army back to warring factions, ripe for the
Bruce's invasion.

"It's for the Bruce," Archie insisted. "We'll get a
ransom on these two for ourselves, though, once we
meet up with the bishop."

"Ransom," muttered the youth, who seemed unable
to raise his voice above that rumble, then he stalked
over to the prisoners and Allyson forced herself to be
still. Anything she could learn from them, by magic or
otherwise, could help her and Robert to escape. "The
English claim no ransom. They slaughter the knights
and hang out the ladies in cages. Less'n they want to
show us what they really think—then they slaughter
the lot, men, women and children." He slashed his hand
out as if cutting down Robert and Allyson both. She
flinched. "My sister and mother among them. Strangled
me and left me for dead."

Close to, Allyson could see the scarred band that
circled his throat.

He ran his hand down one of her braids, hefting it in
his palm. "Are you anybody's mother?"

His breath misted her cheek. "No," she whispered.

"Pity. We might've had to spare you then."

At her side, Robert growled, glaring at the youth,
and Archie stood up, sliding the strap of the satchel
over his shoulder as he approached. "Look, you, Abban,
she's how we get him to pay heed. I know you're that

broke up about your mum, but we're not going to—"

Robert shot to his feet, grabbing the strap of his bag and slamming his head into Archie's, spinning him about and snatching the knife from his belt. Allyson dove out of the way and scrambled up as Robert back-handed the blade into Abban's stomach, jerking it upward with a spray of blood, and turned it back toward Archie. Before he could skewer his next Scotsman, Ivor was on him, swinging his axe.

Dodging the first blow, Robert deflected the torch that bobbed perilously close to his face with his knife-hand. "Run, my lady!" he bellowed.

As if she would leave him there, fighting for both their lives. She darted in toward the dying boy and slid the knife from his sheath though his bloody hands left his wound long enough to try to grapple with her.

The huge cook grabbed one of her braids, pulling her backward, but Allyson magically sent her own disgust rippling along her skin and down her hair, projecting her horror and magnifying the nausea that gripped her stomach. With a gasp, the cook let go and she found her footing, then cried out, "Robert!"

As Archie grappled with his own knife in Robert's hand, Ivor's ax aimed for the knight's chest, a close blow powered by all his strength and hatred.

Allyson sprang forward, barely reaching the Scot's boot as she fell headlong, but it was enough. Her body tingled with power, her own momentum translated from her body to his.

Ivor skidded, crying out as his leg wrenched to the side. Robert desperately pivoted and the ax struck him full-on, but twisted sideways, a crushing blow against his ribs from the flat of the blade. Bones cracked, Robert's eyes flaring over the band that sealing his mouth, and his knees buckled. Even as he fell, she hacked at Ivor's arm, forcing him back.

Already, Archie reclaimed his knife, howling his rage.

Again, the ax struck, still flailing, the handle in Ivor's fist slamming into Allyson's arm. She shrieked, watching with despair as her stolen blade flew free and bounced into the grass. Her arm went numb, her hand dangling, trembling. Allyson let herself fall, let her body interpose between Archie's knife and Robert's prone form, her own weight adding to his burden, her own hands up, cut and bleeding, her left hand finally closing over Archie's as he tried to stab Robert past her shoulder.

"No," she said, "you need him. Remember? You need him. For the Bruce." She flooded the contact with whatever resolve remained to her, a sense of calm she did not feel, a return to reason that even she did not believe in.

Archie's face dripped sweat and blood onto her own, his breathing rasping at her, echoing Robert's struggle to draw breath. Robert's heart thundered at her back, as if it occupied her own ribcage, twin to the heart that beat there for him.

"Bitch," Archie snarled, but he jerked away from her, the madness leaving his eyes, Ivor and the cook coming to loom over their prisoners. "You'll pay for Abban's death, you English devil."

Allyson rolled away, sliding her numbed right arm under Robert's head, her left hand drawing away the gag, barely able to command the magical aid she conjured. He gasped and coughed, she stroked his face, murmuring, close enough to kiss him, his dark eyes blinking back the tears of his agony. Her magical knowledge gave her some insight into the body, but only enough to be think he would not die, and it hardly took a witch to recognize the cracked ribs at his right side.

"Forgive me, lady," he breathed, barely audible. "I failed you."

"No," she whispered back. "You fought bravely, but the odds were against you." Even as she said it, she imagined how it might have gone differently, if Robert had been patient, if the two of them had been able to work together. Instead, he took it on himself to save them, acting rashly. Knowledge was the first law of magic, and knowledge required patience. There would be another chance. There must be.

"You and your fool ideas," Ivor snapped, examining Abban's body. "Can't the bloody grail even heal him?"

Leaving the cook with his cleaver held at the level of Robert's throat, Archie went over to kneel by the fallen youth, but the vacant stare and gaping mouth made it all too clear that he was dead. "Course it heals! Why else—but it don't raise from the dead. Won't bring him back from his rightful place at the hand of God." He reached out to close Abban's eyes and crossed himself.

"I say, kill them now and let the bishop sort out if it's the Grail. It's too risky bringing them anyplace."

"He makes a point," said the cook, his voice low and gruff. "Conspirin' already, aren't they?"

"If you hadn't tipped the cart, Malcolm, we'd've had

no trouble to bring them." Archie sat back on his heels. "Get them separated and get them bound."

Malcolm's fat fingers dug into Allyson's shoulder as he dragged her up and away, Robert's eyes locked to hers until they'd gone beyond him. She winced as the cook squeezed her injured arm, pushing her against one of the standing stones. With the twitch of a thick eyebrow, Malcolm pulled the narrow golden wedding ring from her finger and tucked it into a pouch at his waist. Silent, he bent her arms one at a time around the broad rock, binding her wrists behind it, a length of rope stretched between them, her arm throbbing. The rough stone scraped every bit of exposed skin and her strained shoulders shot her with pain at every breath.

At the center of the clearing, Ivor kicked Robert hard, and again, forcing him onto his injured side, face to face with the corpse of Abban.

"The Grail knows who is worthy," Robert whispered, earning himself another kick as Ivor wrenched his arms back to bind them. "It's the cup of God. Won't just—"

Ivor tore a strip from the boy's bloody tunic and stuffed it in Robert's mouth. He bound Robert's ankles as well and stooped to retrieve the silver fillet that had tumbled from Allyson's hair, flashing it before Robert's eyes. "Just you wait, English. When the bishop gets here, I'll rape your mistress on Abban's corpse and gut you just like you did to him. You'll fuckin' drown in each other's blood."

The fury in his voice chilled Allyson straight through. She tried again to attune herself to this place, but every tiny breath brought pain, Robert's tonsured head bent before that of the dead boy, as if Ivor's threat had already brought him low.

"Won't get no ransom if you kill 'em," Malcolm said mildly, not revealing the ransom he'd already taken from Allyson's finger. He looked her over carefully, sliding a finger along her collarbone to pluck out the thong she wore with its little icon of the Virgin Mary. A trifle, deliberately worthless, and he dropped it back again. As he turned away, Allyson let out a tiny breath of relief. That embroidered icon, made up of scraps from her first bridal gown, her father's shroud, her sister's hair, its Sacred Heart stitched with threads stained red in her own blood—it was her talisman, endowed with an echo of her power to amplify magic. Its loss would reduce her once more to merely a woman, fragile, easily dismissed. No one, not even her first husband, had made her remove it. Randall merely asked her to wear it reversed when he came to her bed, as if he did not wish his lovemaking to be witnessed by the Holy Virgin.

The bishop. More Scots were coming, and she had no way of knowing when or how many. No matter how ill-advised Robert's action, it was true they had little time to effect their escape. As she worked once more for attunement, she allowed her senses to extend through the standing stone, down through the earth, unfurling her awareness to envelope the landscape around her. Three stones, tall, ancient, cold, rough land beyond them, a land of more rock than trees. Ahead of her, thin forest marched down the slope they had climbed to get here, just enough trees to shelter this place and hide it from the road. The tumult of the fight had frightened away whatever creatures might have sheltered there as well. The torch smoldered to one side, thrust upright into the earth, pitch and smoke tainting the air.

With her awareness spread like a net into the world around her, Allyson turned her attention to the others, whose lives disturbed the night like stones dropped into a pool. Malcolm stood at ease, a stolid presence neither fervent as Archie nor furious as Ivor. These latter two had slight injuries, annoyances rather than hindrances, while Robert, lay at their feet, his presence sharp with pain, then ragged as if his strength ebbed away. Three men, then, and all for her to master, alone and unarmed, somehow to diminish them so severely that she could escape with the wounded Robert, who could hardly be counted on for aid. As she gathered herself for some sorcery she could not yet define, she felt a new ripple — someone was coming, a familiar presence, and another, and a dread so tangible she found it hard to catch her breath. Her limbs trembled and she longed for the blanket shed down below, for the familiar warmth and roughness of wool drawn close about her, protecting her, shielding her eyes from whatever came next.

"Hey-up!" called a voice from the forest.

"A watch," Ivor snapped, springing toward the path, axe in hand, taking a fighting stance. "Archie, next time you take control, you think about setting a watch."

Archie, too, brought out his weapon, darting a glance at Ivor, but calling out softly, "Who goes?"

"A friend o' the Bruce, bringin' a present fro' the English."

Ivor spat. "We want nothing of theirs."

"Oh, aye, but ye'll like this." The newcomer approached, a hooded lantern in one hand, and a bundle in the other. "I. . .collected it down the road a bit. On its way back to the castle, I'll warrant." He grinned.

"Donald! Where's Lachlan?"

"He went to hurry the bishop. Given what I've got here, it seemed we might need a hint 'o speed." Donald loped into the light—another kitchen scullion Allyson recognized, and she thought dizzily that Eleanor had been right: the kitchen help were indeed Scotch traitors.

"Damn—they killed Abban? Tha's no' right!" Donald scowled down at their dead companion, then at Robert. "Guess I've evened that score, eh?"

Then Donald gave a little toss, holding one end of the blanket he carried so the rest unwound, sending the contents tumbling to the ground in a spatter of red and a mess of dark curls. By the time she acknowledged what it was, Allyson's throat burned with bile, her stomach rejecting her dinner. The thing rolled to bump against the next standing stone, lifeless eyes staring upward from the disembodied head. Silvio.

ALLYSON'S WAIL of grief struck Randall like a bolt. The more so when it cut off a moment later, and, for a long heartbeat, he feared the worst. Then a muffled sobbing took its place—she was gagged, then, not dead, thank God. For a moment, he lay where he was, a stone among stones, breathing tight, clutching one of the swords at his belt, for courage if nothing else, his forehead resting on the hard earth.

After a time, he forced himself back into motion, desperate to know what had caused her shriek, dreading the idea that he already knew—that Robert was slain before her eyes, before Silvio had had a chance to reach the castle and bring back aid. Pushing away such thoughts, Randall crept forward, keeping low among the stones, barely daring to breathe. The stones gave way to a few straggling trees from the woods that mounted the other side, and Randall kept moving, heading for the sound of a woman's grief, still low beneath the rumble of voices.

"—passed by two horsemen, and we came back up on the road. Only one of them rode back that way, the other man riding on more slow, mayhap following their new Edward, but I misdoubt it."

Randall gripped the tree before him with his fingertips. He did not understand all that they said, but they'd seen Silvio, and himself. The two men from the kitchen must have heard the riders coming and dodged into the trees before Randall had seen them. If he turned now and hurried back the way he had come, he might escape notice, at least long enough to send his horse on without him and perhaps evade a search, but Allyson's muffled sobbing drew him onward even as he prayed to the Virgin that he'd be so close they would miss him.

"Ivor and Donald, you search the hill, and make it thorough—won't do to be surprised when the bishop arrives."

As they grumbled and clomped off to do their master's bidding, one of them cracking through tree branches to the left, the other cursing stones to the right, Randall gripped his swords like a madman to keep them clanking against anything and sped the last few steps. Three great stones loomed in shadow before him, outlined by the feeble light of the torch within the circle—and round one of them stretched a rope that bound a woman's hands.

His heart pounded in his throat and Randall sank down below the shadows of the stones, sliding in behind where she was bound, pressing himself between the tall rock and a smaller one at its back. He stood against it, likely echoing her own posture on the other side, counting on his dark cloak to conceal him from a casual glance. His fingers followed the rope, until they found her wrist.

At the touch, her fingers spasmed and her breath caught with a little choking sound, and he nearly withdrew, but she gave a little moan, fingers wiggling, and he cradled her smaller hand into his palm, a touch more warm and intimate than any they had shared for months.

"My lord, you're here."

Her voice whispered through him, as if at his ear, but he already knew she could not speak. He flinched, but kept his grip, and her words hurried over him. *"Please do not let go, my lord, I beg of you."*

Her voice stirred through him, flesh and bone. "Witches," he breathed. "You and your kinsman both."

"Yes, yes, but not evil—please believe me!"

Her urgency pricked his skin, adding weight to her words, his cheek pressed against the stone, grateful that he had something to prop him up. His wife, a witch. Why hadn't she used her accursed powers to get Robert to fall in love with her, then? "Where's Robert? Does he live?"

"Injured—ribs cracked—bound hand and foot at the center of the clearing. There were four men, two have gone to

search, for you, I guess."

Two men remaining, and Randall had surprise on his side. If he would risk his life for a witch and the man she loved. Did it change anything, this new knowledge? He wished he could confront her right then and rage upon her as he had never done before, and he remembered what she said of Henry, her first husband, visiting his rages upon his child-bride. Did it change anything? It filled him heart and soul with questions, questions only she could answer — and only if she lived.

With his free hand, Randall unclasped his cloak.

"Wait — give me a moment before you attack," she said into his hand.

He gave her fingers another squeeze of acknowledgement, then pushed a little back from the stone, letting his cloak slide to the ground, silently drawing the broadsword he carried for Silvio and cutting the bonds at her wrists. She let her hands remain in position, as if still tied, though her arms must ache. Clever witch. Beautiful, too. If she had cared for him at all, he might well imagine himself the man ensorcelled. Switching the shorter blade to his left hand, Randall slid free his own sword, shifting ever so slightly back. Between the standing stone and the next was a gap wide enough. Two steps and he could be there. The tension of battle slid through his body, flushing out any concerns about Allyson or even Robert. With sword in hand, he could afford concentration on nothing but this, waiting for his moment to attack.

Allyson made a series of distinct sounds, almost conversational.

"Go see what she wants, Malcolm. If she shouts or

gives another shriek like that, cut out her tongue. We can still get a ransom—and likely her husband don't care for her tongue in any case, less'n she uses it right." The speaker laughed, while another man crossed toward Allyson, and her husband tensed, putting off the crude image. No, she would not use her tongue in service of his pleasure, but now he thought of her tears as he touched her—the tears of a woman betrayed and brutalized by her first husband. He should have recognized it before now. He brought the tip of his sword up to his lips, the kiss of cold steel reminding him of his purpose.

"Thank you, Malcolm," Allyson whispered after a moment of throat-clearing.

"What's that? I'll not cut your tongue for speaking a little louder."

Clever indeed. She had separated her guards, and brought one of them within reach. "I can't, my throat is so very dry," she whispered, again hardly above a breath. Her fingers gave a flicker that Randall caught from the corner of his eye, a tiny gesture sending him on. And on he came.

Randall pounced, pivoting around the stone as Allyson snatched back her arm and dove to the side. A large man in an apron stood facing her, turning to watch her dodge away, starting to shout. Randall's blade sliced into his back, chinked into bone, driving the man with all of his strength against the stone.

Back arching, mouth gaping with blood, Malcolm slammed the stone. As Randall drew back the blade, his enemy crumpled to the ground, back broken, blood streaming, face twisting in pain.

One. Randall turned, two blades held. Robert, bound

at the center, next to a dead man, another man standing over them, briefly dumfounded, then drawing his knife, dropping the bag he carried, Robert's bag. The hundred details fusing like stained glass, into the window he needed to view the battle. If he could draw on the other guard, but the man lunged for Robert instead, only the corpse interfering with his taking a hostage.

Three long strides, sword already up, on guard, the second weapon coming in low beneath it. The Scot fell back at the sight of him, shouting, "Ivor! Donald! To me!"

As he leapt the two prone forms, Randall dropped his left-hand weapon and drew his dagger. "My lady — get him free!"

The sounds of movement, a cry of assent, his sword clanging against the other man's long knife. It would be a very short fight. He slid his sword upward, swinging the other man's blade with it, exposing his own side, if the other man had had another blade. He did not. Randall's dagger thrust, but the Scot twisted and dropped away, retreating as Randall's weapon sliced his tunic.

Sounds persisted behind him, hard to separate, aside from Allyson's low, soothing voice. He advanced again toward the floundering Scot, and noted the flick of his eyes, the flash of a smile that ghosted his opponent's lips.

Randall ducked and turned, sword coming about as an axe plunged toward him. The blow, which would have taken his shoulder at the neck, smashed into his sword. His feet skidded and held.

"Thank God!" The first man spat somewhere behind him.

With a twist, Randall let his sword arm drop, bringing up the dagger, but the Scot's thick kilt flared as he spun away, rounding for another stroke of the axe. If even one blow landed, unarmored as he was, Randall would lose a limb, if not his life.

This opponent, taller, lean, with a cleft chin, bared his teeth and charged.

At times, on the fields of Scotland where rough, common folk like these men confronted the well-armed and armored cavalry of England, Randall almost regretted the slaughter, admiring the charismatic leaders, Wallace and now Bruce, who had brought such a rabble together and given them tactics to face the greatest army in the world. Here, on foot, Randall felt only thanks to God for his own skill.

He side-stepped the torch planted in the earth, and feinted right, hoping to draw off the man's weapon, but the Scot snarled and drove toward him instead.

At the corner of his eye, he caught the movement of the second Scot, trying to slip behind him. "Aye—tha'll be him, I reckon!" called the voice of Donald, charging back up the right-hand slope.

Two yes, but not three, not without even a shield, with two potential hostages or targets in his protection. "Robert!"

"Yes, my lord!" Robert's voice, weak and wheezing. Bad—very bad.

"Can you fight?"

A hesitation. "Yes, my lord." A lie, or a promise. Robert was a good knight, a good man, a good friend: he would fight at Randall's word or die trying.

Randall spun a quick half-circle, fending off the

knife, but the ax swung down while he was open. He stumbled, something tripping him up, and fell briefly to his knees, the ax carving a swath of air where his chest had been a moment ago, the breeze of it slapping his face. Getting a foot under him, Randall launched himself toward the standing stones, taking a slice that stung along his spine.

He spun about, placing his bleeding back to the rock.

Across the clearing, Robert struggled to his feet, his right side clearly bent, his left hand clutched about himself in some effort at supporting the broken ribs as he lifted the sword Randall had dropped for him. Allyson knelt there still, dropping the straps which had bound him, her face pale and stricken, her hair loose of its braids, splashed with blood he hoped did not belong to her.

Shouts echoed from the slope toward the road with the rushing of many men. In spite of the two men facing him, the third closing in on his friend, Randall felt a surge of hope as reinforcements arrived.

Flinging up his defenses, Randall blocked the axe, chinking its wooden handle then he caught sight of the thing that had tripped him. Silvio's disembodied head. There would be no aid from the castle; the reinforcements were not for him.

"Holy Mary, Mother of God," Robert's voice grew stronger as he prayed, even between the grunts and winces of his pain as he struggled to fend off Donald's knife and axe.

"Don't let her get the Grail!" the older man squeaked.

The Grail? What was he on about?

The ax clanged the stone by his head, deafening.

Some of the newcomers appeared through the trees, bearing a few lanterns, pointing, shouting though Randall could not hear them. No more could he hear Robert's desperate prayer, though his own lips moved in unison with his memory. Dead. They would all be dead in a matter of seconds, and he had never told Allyson the truth. It would take a miracle to save them now. Still, he did not stop fighting.

He landed a slice across the Scot's thigh that briefly pushed him back, and searched for a glimpse of his wife.

Allyson rose at the center of the clearing, and a great light spread around her, colored by gemstones, reflecting in gold. It cast its glow upon her face and made her radiant, turning the bloodstains on her gown to mere shadows, carrying an unseen fire. She was a vision from the tales of Arthur, the Grail-maiden come to life, standing, glowing there among them, putting all their might and fury to shame with the glory of herself and the thing she carried.

"Hold," she cried in a voice resonant with power. "Hold in the name of the Father, and the Son, and the Holy Spirit. Lower your arms in the presence of the Grail!"

ALLYSON HELD the Grail before her, drawing all of her strength, all of her will, all of her need into this moment. As a girl, she learned to use her magic cautiously lest she or her mother be found out. It was useful, the aid in healing, the listening, the knowing of things that others knew not, but never before had her life depended on it.

She forced all trembling from her limbs, all terror from her voice, and schooled herself to holiness, to be what she would have them see. From the astonished stares of the newcomers, from the blade that dropped from Robert's tired grasp and the failure of his opponent to slay him, Allyson knew it was working.

She turned a slow circle, not letting her gaze rest too long on any one man, but fixing each of them in turn. His back to the stone, Randall held off two assailants, blood streaming down his arm, his dark eyes flicking toward her, flaring wide, then fixed once more on his enemies.

While she and the ladies stitched and spoke and read in the hall at Carlisle or their own halls back at home, these men rode out to battle, day after day, at the command of their king. She had seen them practice, had tended minor wounds for one husband or the other, had seen the paintings and tapestries of great battles, and even stitched a few such scenes herself, but never before had she seen the truth of such a thing.

All the strength of Randall's muscular shoulders and powerful arms—the strength she feared that he, like Henry, would turn against her— all the sharp concentration of those dark eyes focused on this, the efficient assault of his enemies. If Robert were not so tired and so wounded, he would surely fight with such economy and grace, drawing his opponents away from the innocent, choosing his place, moving without anger and without haste, transforming the battle into a sort of deadly dance from which, if their enemies had not just conjured themselves twenty more men, Randall would emerge with a flourish over the bodies of his enemies laid low before him.

Instead, three more men rushed up, spears in hand. While he fought off the ax and the knife, any single spear could stab through his defenses. Even so, he did not quail before them, his lips moved in a silent prayer, his being focused on a fight which must be to the death, a death which must be, given the growing odds, his own.

Allyson shifted her feet, touching the base of the torch, and sent her strength along that shaft which burst to life in a shower of sparks. She forged an affinity between these lights and the gems on the cup she carried, and made a cascade of lights in emerald, sapphire and pearl. "Hold!" she cried again, raising the grail above her head, and a second voice joined hers.

"Hold, you knaves! and kneel!"

Archie stumbled toward her, his face gone slack, his eyes drawn toward the heavens, then he sank to his knees. Behind him, one of the spearmen threw his weapon. Randall twisted away, dodging the spear, but trapping his sword arm as Ivor pressed his advantage.

Randall's knees buckled--by injury or design, she could not say--his dagger upthrust, piercing Ivor's chest. The ax tumbled, the flat struck Randall's head a hard blow, the edge carved along his back until it finally fell with its master. Staggered against the stone, Randall propped himself with a shaky hand. Still breathing, still blinking through the blood that streamed down his scalp. It shook her, to see him fallen in the height of his strength, her throat more dry than ever. He deserved a better end than to pursue his faithless wife into a battle he did not own.

"Kneel, I say, in the name of your king, if not of the

Lord above!" A man in flowing robes and embroidered cap pushed through the arrested rabble of Scots, holding up a cross of gold from the chain around his neck.

His men slowly obeyed, even Donald leaving off his attack, perhaps disarmed by the fact that Robert was already kneeling, hands pressed together in prayer, gazing raptly up as if Allyson had become the Holy Virgin herself.

She let the last of the sparks fall.

Archie crowed, "You see, Your Grace? It is the Grail! Surely Lachlan told you! We're saved — the Bruce need suffer no longer."

At the bishop's side, another man, kneeling, frowned, a ring upon his fisted hand winking in the glow of the Grail: another of the servants of Carlisle castle. "We can't be sure. We can't simply take the word — "

"Hush, Lachlan," said the bishop, looking over the strange assembly. Allyson imagined how it must seem, two bloodied English knights, a flaxen-haired woman of clear Saxon descent, the glowing cup in her hands, the corpses of Scottish soldiers. "Whence came the grail, Lady, if you will say?"

"It was carried by the hand of this holy knight, come to our land to serve those in need and worthy of its aid."

"Oh, we're worthy, aye," Archie whispered.

The bishop crossed himself and rose, approaching her, his blue eyes gleaming with the reflected glory. "May I, Lady? May I examine it?"

Allyson's own ribs felt too tight, constricting her breath and her voice. There must be a way to turn this moment to their freedom. She lowered the cup, removing one hand, but not the other, allowing him to touch the Grail, but only at the touch of her own hand as she twined her power through the contact, gently, gently. The transactions of magic were nearly impossible against the will of any creature with mind to defy it, but as a tool for learning, for understanding men and what their will might do, it was invaluable.

"Your servants have said that you would bring this to the Bruce himself," she murmured, keeping her voice warm, sensing the devout faith of the man before her. The strong current of truth echoed that faith. "The Grail is no weapon, Your Grace. It may not be used in force of arms."

"No, certainly not," he murmured, his trembling fingers tracing its rim and stroking over its jewels.

She wet her lips, bracing herself for her next foray. "Then I cannot see that the Bruce is worthy to receive it."

"Victory is not his only need, Lady," said the bishop, very softly, hope heating his touch. For a moment, she felt the echoes of another, a man very close to this one, a supplicant, a confessed sinner, a man who would be king of his people, a man who lost feeling in a few fingers, who noticed patches of graying skin.

Allyson formed the word within herself, and dare not speak it aloud, the curse that could ruin a king and bring down his half-won kingdom if such rumors passed. She let her skin speak her guess, with all the weight and agony of truth. "*Leprosy.*"

The bishop reeled, gasping and snatching back his hand from the cup, his eyes gleaming now with sudden tears. "Did you hear that?"

"I hear the prayers of many," Allyson replied.

Crossing himself warily, glancing up, then bringing his gaze back upon her, the bishop said, "What must we do, Lady, to prove the worth of our cause?"

"Forgive me, Your Grace," said Lachlan, rising as well and stalking toward them. "How can we be sure this is the. . . what you claim it is? You cannot bargain for a golden cup and a pretty girl."

"She is not part of any bargain," said Randall, limping up beside her, his hand upon his sword hilt, the weapon lightly sheathed. So near, she heard the ragged course of his breathing after the fervor of his words.

"She is the vessel through which the Grail makes its power known," said Robert, reverently, gazing up at her, not rising though his hands had left the attitude of prayer and returned to cradling his injured side, his handsome face caught between faith and pain.

"Forgive me, Lady," Archie muttered, and his sudden contrition after hours of enduring his bold talk made her want to laugh or let loose some flare of punishing power. Still, if she would convince them that only the worthy could handle the Grail, then she could not afford any sign of anger or offense.

Randall drew himself up, mustering some dignity beneath the blood and mess of battle. "We may be prepared, on behalf of the Order of the Knights Templar, and of the Kingdom of England, to negotiate your use of the Grail," Randall announced, "if there is one among you with such authority."

"There's only three of them, Your Grace," Lachlan pointed out. "We've no need to negotiate at all." His black stare made his meaning clear.

Allyson drew upon her strength, the talisman of the

Virgin that she wore at her throat and the talisman she held in her hands fairly vibrating with power as she called up the blood that stained her hands and gown, the blood of her own scrapes and scratches, and let it creep along her arms, dripping down from the golden cup like bloody tears. "It weeps," she shrieked, raising it again over her head so that all could see, then clutching it to her breast like a baby in need of comfort. "It weeps to know the violence in your heart."

Lachlan, taken aback, stammered, "I'm sure there's violence in many hearts."

The bishop clutched his man's shoulder as a murmur spread among the soldiers. "Lachlan, your doubts do credit to your loyalty, but one cannot tempt the blessings of the Lord."

Robert gave a quiet groan and Allyson heard him fall. Tension flowed through her body. She longed to drop beside him, to cast off the stupid cup, the foolish and dangerous charade she had begun, take Robert's poor head in her lap and ease his pain.

Randall's strong hand rested upon her arm. "Indeed not, Your Grace, and we can see your faith commands you to believe. But there are those among your people who will not trust in faith alone."

Through the contact, Allyson felt his own fear and tension, almost felt the questions he wanted to ask, tingling shallow at the surface, and, underlying these, a near-impenetrable wall that took all of his effort to sustain. The pulse of his pain distracted her, but she framed her words for him, sending through the contact they shared. *"The Bruce has leprosy — only the bishop knows, and perhaps a handful of others. I have to —"* but she bit off that last, struggling to conceal her own anguish, knowing Robert lay beside her, unable to give in to the womanly feelings that threatened to overwhelm her. Keeping the worries from her face, Allyson sent her words, her desperate pleading. *"Robert is injured. If I can touch him, I can help him to heal."*

Randall registered surprise at her news about the Bruce, worry over his friend, a shaft of sadness, but he projected strength, a skill almost as practiced as the art of the magus. "Among the legendary powers of the Grail is healing, is it not? Our companion is grievously wounded. I believe that, with the aid of the Grail, he can be healed."

"Please take no offense, my lord, but how do we know he's worthy? If it fails on an unworthy recipient, it is no true test, and this is a fighting man, doubtless with many sins upon his soul."

Allyson flared in righteous anger on Robert's behalf, the Grail glinting as she strengthened the light it gathered.

Randall's hand remained calm. "As, I am sure, would be those you would aid with its presence, but it was he who was chosen to bring the Grail here, for his battles are fought in the name of the Lord."

"How is such a thing to be done?" the bishop inquired, spreading his hands.

"Water," Allyson blurted, then got her tone back under control. "Water or wine, taken from the cup."

Lachlan held up a wineskin, his doubts writ plain upon his features.

Randall released his sword at last, letting it slide home with a distinct sound and gesture that could be read as either a promise or a threat. He took the skin and unstoppered it, pouring a draught into the Grail, gazing at Allyson over the rim. She turned away once this was done and knelt at Robert's side, freeing one hand to take his head into her lap. Attuning herself to him was a matter of simply drawing a breath in his presence, drawing up the love she bore for him, her gratitude for his kindnesses, her desire for his notice. He groaned softly.

Magic could not be forced upon someone, but healing was another matter. Body and spirit alike longed to be whole and healthy. The magus could focus her will to encourage it, using the affinity of her own uninjured body to reflect the image of health. A simple healing, as it was called, could be cast by any with power, possessing only the knowledge of that basic desire for health. It was not painless, nor instantaneous, but it was what she could offer him, and Allyson conjured it now, cradling his head and shoulders, bringing the Grail to his lips.

Briefly, he tried to resist, his lips mumbling, protesting his unworthiness. And that humility, of course, was what made him so supremely worthy after all. Tears burned at Allyson's eyes as she encouraged him, all of her being, her power, her presence, bent upon this—that he should be healed.

At last, she tipped the cup, allowing him to swallow a few gulps, then a few more. He leaned his head back with a sigh, his hand resting on her arm, the other lying at the cross upon his chest, and she could feel the prayer he recited in his heart.

She focused her thoughts upon his battered ribs,

cracked first by the axe's blow, then stove in by Ivor's wicked boot. She winced as her own ribs ached in sympathy, then Robert screamed, his back arching, and sagged against her, shaking, then drawing a breath that did not hitch in pain.

Robert's eyes flashed open, and he gasped, laughed, blinked up at her. "My lady!" Even his eyes had lost that rim of exhaustion he carried home from France, that must have haunted him since he had left the presence of his Grand Master. "I—it is a miracle." He prodded his side with one hand, grinning in wonder. "Praise be to God."

His brows flared, a sudden rush of shame flooding him, and he fumbled away, sitting up, vacating her lap, his cheeks reddening, especially as he glanced toward Randall who stood looking on with the whole of the Scottish party. "My lord. Forgive me," Robert began, but Randall put up his hand for peace.

Randall started to shake his head, but winced, eyes sliding shut and open again, the left side of his head still oozing blood.

"Sir knight, what do you feel?" the bishop leaned in, peering at Robert.

"The pain had overcome me, Your Grace, and I felt as if I must die. I lay praying to the Virgin, until—my lady came to me with the cup. I did not, do not, feel worthy of such a gift, and yet." He touched his throat, let his hand trail down to the cross on his tabard. "The wine tasted of blood, Your Grace, and I could feel the heat of it move through me. For a moment, I could feel the. . .the depth of a perfect love." He finished, crossed himself, and bowed his head.

"For the Lord so loved the earth that He gave his only begotten son," the bishop intoned, crossing himself and kissing the crucifix he wore.

"You say you are empowered to negotiate for the Scots, for the Bruce," Randall snapped, swinging away from Robert and forcing the bishop to meet his eyes. "We are willing to negotiate, on behalf of the Templars and the King of England. There must be no more hostilities. No more raids against our borders or attempts to claim the castles we hold."

Lachlan snarled, and even the bishop gave a snort. "You ask much, my lord."

"You are asking us to give over to you the very cup of Christ," Randall replied, his tone echoing with disbelief.

Allyson remained upon the ground, her power all but drained, grateful for the sun that crept into the sky and cast its rosy glow on Robert's cheek. Indeed, he looked well again, returned to the flower of youth and chivalry. At his other side, Randall stood just a little taller than Robert's shoulder, his face intent on his words, as ever giving his full attention to what needed him most.

"Five years," Randall was saying. "At the end of which time, you shall deliver the Grail again to us, and neither side makes guarantee to uphold the truce."

"Five years?" Robert said, "How can you be sure they'll give it back?"

"They are men of honor, are they not? And they shall be made to swear in its very presence, as shall we." He made an imperious motion with his hand, and Allyson rose to her feet, trembling, and managed to walk to him without wobbling too much. He glanced at her, his mouth hardening, and glanced away again. "And we shall need our horses back, plus two more, one of which will carry the body of my wife's kinsman to Carlisle to be received and buried with honor."

"Horses!" Lachlan muttered.

"How vital is it to you, Your Grace," Randall said, but he was staring at Lachlan as he said it, "that the Grail reach your chosen king?"

"Horses. Lachlan, please see to it, and to the loading of the squire's body." The bishop flicked his fingers, and Lachlan rose to do his bidding. "We shall need to write all of this out, to have it sealed both by Bruce and by Edward."

Allyson twitched at the sound of that name, and realized what Randall must already have known: the Scots did not know either that Edward was dead. He was negotiating the peace that Hugh needed in order to cement his own power, the peace that would ensure the safety of the border for the next few years. And who knew but that the Bruce might die of his disease before the truce had even ended? She darted a glance toward Robert, who stood much better healed than she had any right to expect. Was it her own love threading through her magic that healed him? His faith in God and in the Grail? If the Bruce possessed such faith, or had a magus of his own to wield the Grail, would he, too, be healed?

Allyson said, "Sir Robert's things included parchment and ink. The truce might be sworn upon right now by those who represent the combatants."

Randall smiled, the expression made a little one-sided by his wound, then he moved aside with the bishop to discuss the wording of the document they would sign. Robert prowled the clearing, dawn's light now filling the place, the wary Scots whispering among themselves. Lachlan reappeared, leading a horse already laden with a blanket-wrapped form, and taking up Silvio's head to wrap that as well. Allyson shuddered, returning her gaze to Robert as he shifted the body of the dead cook.

Randall came up quietly beside her as she watched. "I know what it is to love without being loved. We have that much in common, anyhow," her husband murmured, and she looked at him, feeling a twinge of remorse at the blood caked on his face. He had brushed against her as he spoke, and she was not sure if he meant to be heard, or if she heard him only through that contact.

"Official copies will come to us from the Bruce in the next few weeks." Blowing out a breath, he held up a document. "Now that I have signed for England, and the bishop for Scotland, they are asking for the Grail."

"Yes, of course." She stared down at the thing in her hands, now only a heavy cup, gilded and bejeweled, its interior dark with ancient shadows.

"Is it real, or was it all your power?"

"My lord," she said, "this power is not a Devil's thing, you must believe me —"

He put up his hand, touched her shoulder and withdrew. "It matters not to me what you are, my lady — what you have always been. If I had trusted you earlier, if I had trusted Silvio, this day might have been very different."

Something melted within her, the defense she

worked so hard to build against him, against any man with the power to hold her, the strength to hurt her, the will to try to break her. He possessed all of those things, and yet, he used them not at all. She gazed at him in astonishment. A denunciation from him, and she could be arrested, imprisoned, executed, with him the beneficiary of all of her lands and titles, free then to marry where he would, shut of her forever. That he would forbear, knowing what she was, told her more about him than ever she had known or wished to know before.

"I should be pleased if you would tell me about your power, if you wish to tell me. If your. . .situation allows." His gaze, too, rested on Robert. "Hugh will grant us an annulment, if I ask him. And that is not the only vow that can be forsaken," he told her, "according to the Pope himself, there is no order of the Temple any more."

Randall put his hand gently over hers and slid the Grail away, hefting its weight, then walked away from her, his body taut with the effort not to show his exhaustion, toward the party of Scots.

Across the bloody grass, Robert approached, carrying something between his fingers, a ring that winked gently in the daylight. He yawned, shook his head, and smiled down at her as he came close and dropped her wedding ring into her palm. "Don't want to leave that to the Scots, my lady, even if we must leave them the Grail."

Allyson frowned down at it. "You've known my husband a long time, Robert."

"I've had the honor to know him since we were

boys, my lady."

"He said," she hesitated, unsure if this were a breach of confidence, then sighed a little and continued, "he said that he knew what it was to love without being loved. Do you know what he meant?"

"Don't you know?" Robert's brows rose, then his eyes tracked to where Randall stood by the forest, watching the Scots take their leave. "No, I don't suppose you do—he's too proud for that. Only one woman he's ever loved, my lady. But she was already married when he saw her first. Two years, he loved her, from afar, as they say."

She shared his rueful smile. "Isn't that how they say it should be, in those books and songs of courtly love?"

"A knight in love above his station, oh, yes, my lady—not that I am one who courts or loves. But him—"a tip of his head—"never could get the lady from his heart, could he? When her husband died, he fell into a fright, thinking it was his own prayers had made it so, wondering what the cost would be. Then he shrugged off the fear and set about to prove to her parents he was worthy of her. Never seen a man try so hard or worry so much." He gave a long, heavy sigh, rubbing the back of his neck.

Allyson, too, studied her husband, his wounds still seeping blood, the weariness of battle showing in the set of his shoulders, the sag of his head, until, with the Scots finally gone, he sank down to one of the stones, forehead propped on one fist, the other hand loose, even shaking a little until he closed it into a fist. His wounds needed tending, and Allyson felt the stab of regret that she had not the strength to work her magic on him as well. Surely, he was just as worthy. He looked older, and yet more vulnerable, as if, now that the risk was passed, he let his guard down at last, as if, in hiding herself from him, she had never, in fact, seen him at all. He carried some deep pain that weighed upon his heart, that much she knew, and maybe Robert's words had finally given her a hint of what it was.

"What happened to her?" Allyson asked.

Robert tipped a finger under her chin, a familiar touch that one time would have sent her into dreamy ecstasy. Robert lost his smile, his touch echoing with regrets of his own as he answered, "My lady, he married her."

Oh, she thought, but did not say. The truth of it settling over her as Robert withdrew his hand, folded his arms, remained there, a solid presence, ever loyal, ever distant—safe, because she need share nothing at all with him but what she willed to share, because his vows and his honor and his utter lack of interest meant he would not touch her. Safe, because she knew he would be miles away, because she knew he was dedicated to another cause completely. Safe. A love she knew she could allow because she risked, in loving him, nothing at all.

All those times that the young Randall visited at Henry's court and she, frightened child that she was, barely noticed him. All those times he called at her parents' manor, inquiring after her health, bringing what few gifts he could afford, wooing them to trust him, before they ever gave him leave to work at wooing her. What had she been to him? Indifferent? Cold? Surely she had never been actively cruel. Not until they married, when she denied his obvious joy, rejected his every kindness, refused him the truth of what had happened to her, refused to trust him in any way, with her mind, her body, her heart. She should have known. Any magus worth the title should have surely seen that her own husband was in love with her.

Allyson pressed her fist to her mouth, the ring burrowing into her palm. How lonely he must have been, all those days beside her, trying every way he could to show her. How lonely she had been, all of those days denying him.

Plucking up her skirt with her other hand, Allyson closed the distance between them, and sank to her knees at his feet. She wanted to touch him, but feared her touch would only bring him more pain, both in his body, slashed by the Scots, and in his heart, which she, herself, had wounded.

"My lord," she said, and he gave a stir, his eyes opening, beneath the shadow of the hand that cradled his brow.

"All settled is it, my lady?" His eyes glinted, his mouth set in a hard line, not of anger, but of dread.

"Randall," she whispered, and opened her palm to reveal the ring.

"Don't give it back," he said, half a moan, staggering up from the stone, exposing his wounded back as if inviting her to add a blow of her own. "I don't want it back."

"I know," she whispered, and he sagged a little further, all his gallant resolve crumpling before her eyes, her strong, proud, level-headed husband going all to pieces.

"He told you," Randall whispered back, throaty and hurt.

"I should have known."

"I have left no ounce of magnanimity, my lady. I have no eloquence nor diplomacy, I have barely a breath of civility left in me after this very, very long night." He wiped his bloody brow with his arm, flinched, and stared at the gash in his sleeve as if surprised to find another injury, then let his hand fall. "Say what you would have of me, lady, and have done."

"I am ashamed of myself, my lord. Ashamed because you stand before me, wounded and bleeding, and I turned away to heal another—and now I have not the strength left to heal you. Ashamed because the deepest wound is that I made myself, when I should have known better."

He made no answer, but vibrated with that pain.

Allyson once more close the distance. She slid her arm around his, pulling herself close to his shoulder, pressing her face against him, for the first time, longing to touch him, to hold him and be held by him in turn.

"*I'm sorry,*" she said, through every inch of contact they shared. "*Forgive me, Randall, for never having seen you until now.*"

"Until you are leaving." His voice choked with despair, and she clung to him all the more.

"No!" she said fiercely. "No, I am not leaving you. I'm asking you to marry me again, to make again those promises we should have shared. This—"she opened her hand before him, the ring twinkling—"this meant the world to you, and I was too scared to see what it could mean to me."

He wrapped her hand inside his own, seizing her fist, crushing his ring inside as he brought her hand to his heart. "You have no reason to be scared, my lady, not of me, not ever. If I had known what he was doing to you, I should have slaughtered him myself. His death seemed the answer to my prayer, and your indifference the punishment for my selfishness." Then he gave a short bark of laughter. "I hope you do not fall in love with every man who rescues you."

"No, my lord. Only two of them."

He bowed his head, for a moment absolutely still. "Two?"

Randall faced her fully at last, his eyes so alight with hope that she laughed in turn, only then noticing that she was crying as well. "Dear God, Allyson, I had so long ago given up even praying."

She stroked his face, smoothing back his hair, tracing his brow, his jaw, meeting his wondering gaze. She felt giddy, foolish, shy and eager all at once. Tangling her fingers through his hair, Allyson trapped their joined hands between them as she pushed up on her toes and kissed him, a kiss tainted with his blood, a kiss that promised he should bleed for her no more. Their hearts beat together in the growing dawn, safe and close and warm.

THE END

Looking for more adventures in medieval England?
Read on for an excerpt from

Elisha Barber (DAW books, 2013), Book One

Book One of The Dark Apostle series, available
wherever books are sold!

CHAPTER 1

"You sent her to the hospital?" Elisha whirled to face
his brother, the razor still in his fist. "My God,
man, what were you thinking?"

"The midwife couldn't help her, Elisha, and she's in
such awful pain, for the babe won't come," Nathaniel
stammered, his pale hands clenched together. He
ducked in the low door of the draper's quarters, his
fair hair brushing the carved oak of the lintel. "The
neighbors carried her over while I came here."

"But the hospital? That place is deadly." Elisha set
his razor again at his customer's chin, deftly shearing
a narrow stretch of the full, and now unfashionable,

beard. "What did she say?

"Not so fast, if you don't mind. I care to keep my chin today, Barber," the draper snapped.

"Helena?" Nathaniel asked, his face a mask of anguish and confusion.

"No, you fool, the midwife!" Elisha slapped the razor through the water basin and plied it again, forcing himself to slow down. Last thing he needed was to carve the ear off the master of the drapers' guild.

Sagging, his brother balanced himself against the wall, scrubbing at his sweaty face. "The babe's turned, and wedged somehow. She thought the physicians—"

At the mention of physicians, Elisha froze. The draper glowered up at him from his best leather chair, but his brother's wife lay in the hospital, contracting God-knew-what illness added to her condition. For a moment, his conflicting duties trapped him—but Helena needed him, if it weren't already too late. The draper could abide. Flinging down his razor, Elisha roughly dried his hands on his britches. "The physicians never enter the hospital if they can advise from afar. Nobody who can afford their services goes to hospital." He popped open the window frame nearest and flung out the dirty water.

The draper rubbed a hand across his chin and jerked it back with a cry of dismay. "You've not finished the job, Barber. I've still got half a beard!"

"Then you owe me half my fee," Elisha told him. He snatched his towel from the man's neck and spun on his heel, basin tucked under his arm. The razor he folded with a snap and gripped until his fingers hurt. "Why did you not come for me sooner?" he asked, dropping his voice to a murmur.

Instantly, Nathaniel straightened, taking advantage of his superior height. "I think you know why."

For a moment, their eyes met, and Nathaniel swallowed but gave no ground to his elder brother. Elisha had caused the breach that lay between them. He had apologized, but Nathaniel's presence here was as close as he would come to forgiveness.

They had the same intense blue gaze, though Elisha's own hair was near black and bound into a practical queue. Elisha straightened broad shoulders and flashed a furious grin. "Then let's be off while your wife yet lives."

Nathaniel stumbled out the door as Elisha bore down upon him.

"I'll be to your order about this!" The draper squawked, pushing himself up. "You'll not practice in this city again."

Rounding on the man, Elisha said, "I hope they'll consider a woman's life of more value than half a beard."

"A whore's life," the draper answered, then stepped back as Elisha held up the razor, still gripped in his fist. His mobile face registered his regret, but Elisha was in no mood to play the draper's game.

"Helena," Elisha said in a low and terrible voice, "is a whore no longer, but you'll be a bugger for the rest of your life, so I'll ask you to keep your threats to yourself."

Pale, the man's jaw dropped, his half-beard bisecting his lips.

As he turned to follow his brother, Elisha thought it a fitting image, half a beard for a man with a double life. No, the order would hear of nothing from him for a variety of reasons.

Anger was easy. It gave Elisha the distance he needed from those he must treat — and those who might die. Distance, too, from dangerous friends. Elisha would have to apologize at some point, but the draper would be a little more careful suggesting his attraction to his next barber. It would be safer for them both.

Elisha descended the narrow stairs at a run, jumping the last few to street level, emerging between the draper's shop and the neighboring woolery. Nathaniel hovered anxiously in the street, turning away toward the hospital, but only after the relief showed plain upon his face.

Elisha might have found that expression of relief touching at another time, a time when he was more certain of his skill. As it stood, he'd not dealt much with childbirth, though he'd had more experience with it than most barbers, in the course of his work as the favored surgeon of Codpiece Alley. And even there, many of the whores forbore to accept the service of a man, or would take advice only but no examination. Curious, that they who spent their love at the whim of strangers should turn prudish when it came to the touch of an examiner's hand. Most at least knew the herbs to take to avoid unwanted children, else they were cast out by their keepers to give birth in the streets — or, heaven forbid, in the hospital. Elisha's fury flared again. His brother should have known better.

They slogged along the twisting roads of the drapers' quarter, dodging customers, wagons and horsemen, speaking not a word. Nathaniel stuck his shaking hands under his arms, as if he embraced himself in his wife's absence. He still wore his leather tinsmith's apron, the pockets bristling with tools and bits of metal. The midwife must've fetched him up from the workshop. What was he making that was so important he left his wife to birth in the hands of strangers? If Helena had been Elisha's own wife — but, of course, she wasn't. Not his wife, not his choice.

As if he could hear his brother's thoughts, Nathaniel suddenly said, "I couldn't bear the screaming, nor the tears. I waited at the door, I did, but I couldn't bear to hear her like that."

The buildings loomed over them, stepping out from the lower stories until the levels above bent together and cut the sky into jagged shapes. In some places rods and arches touched buildings on both sides of the street, holding apart the tilting houses like a man intervening in a tavern brawl. The graveled streets twined between, edged by ditches to catch rain and refuse. Straight ahead, the carriage of some fool lord had broken a wheel. Two matched horses whinnied and pulled in opposite directions while the grooms tried to sort them out, unhitching the pair and effectively blocking the road while their master shouted from the safety of the carriage. It was just a few years ago King Hugh commissioned carriages for his family. Now every noble who could afford it had to have one, cluttering up the London streets.

With a yelp, Nathaniel stopped short, his shoulders quivering. Elisha grabbed his arm and jerked him forward again, taking to the sewage ditch that ran down the side and ducking beneath the tangled reins. "Pull yourself together, Nate, it's your family at stake," he muttered, not sure if he wanted to be heard.

The hospital at last towered before them, a story of stone at street level, topped with two more of half-timbers spanned by crumbling plaster, with birds plucking out the insulating straw for nests, or in search of insects. It was founded by the old king at the turn of the century and already decrepit. Nowadays, the current king's reputation hardly hewed to charity.

"Which ward?" Elisha asked as they entered the place. Even the refuse he scraped off his boots didn't smell so foul as the hall they faced. The scents of infection, vomit, and blood hung in the air, along with the groans, prayers, and weeping of the afflicted.

"Three?" Nathaniel suggested.

Tension gathering in his shoulders, Elisha focused a brief glare upon his brother, then pushed by him. "Sister!"

A nun passing with a bucket turned at his call. "May I . . . ? Oh." Her wide brown eyes flooded with tears.

"Is it Helena?" Nathaniel blurted, but Elisha held him back, recognizing in the woman before him an emaciated whore he had given a cure four winters back. She had sworn off the life—they all swear off it some time or another—but this oath had taken hold, and he smiled as she dropped the bucket to catch his bare forearm.

"May the Lord bless you, Elisha, and keep you in His hand."

"Sister . . ." he paused, squeezed his eyes shut, and popped them open, "Lucretia?"

She rewarded him with a nod.

"Do you remember Helena? Was she brought in

here?"

"Helena? Gracious, no, I should hope not. Upstairs maybe. Follow!" Gathering up her skirts, Lucretia set a brisk pace for the stairs at the center of the ward.

Averting his eyes from the whimpering or wailing occupants of the broad beds, Elisha followed. After a moment, he thought to look back and caught hold of Nathaniel's arm once more as his brother staggered, his face gray. "Come on, Nate."

"Is it—?"he gasped for breath, recoiling from the stink, "is it always like this?"

"It's worse in the summer," Elisha replied grimly.

Flicking him a glance, Nathaniel looked on the verge of tears himself. "I sent Helena here."

Since Nathaniel's appearance at the draper's, Elisha had felt disconcerted, allowing his brother's agitation to affect him. He'd overreacted, treating Nathaniel with less affection than he would have shown a stranger. He held Nathaniel's arm, lending him strength, as if he could communicate his apology through touch. "You've never been inside the place before. How could you know?"

"By the cross, Elisha, I could have trusted your stories."

Aye, that he could. "What reason have you to trust me, Nate?" Elisha said lightly, despite the heaviness in his heart. A ward sister met them on the landing and pointed toward the far end of the hall. A curtain there separated the wards, and the trio pushed through, pausing briefly at each bed.

Six beds lined the walls, each double width and filled with three or four women. Some of them writhed with unknown pains, moaning or cursing. At the sight of Lucretia, those who could, sat up, holding out beseeching arms.

"Sister, some water, I beg you," cried a crone with sallow flesh.

A better dressed woman in a bed of her own shouted, "Damn you, I need fresh linens!"

One piteous voice whispered, "Just a strip. I'll bind the wound myself, Sister, if you'll give me a bandage." The girl held close a ragged hand, blood streaming from an unseen wound.

Gritting his teeth, Elisha pressed his forearms over his ears, trying to block out their cries. If only he had time. "Helena!" he shouted over the din. "Helena! Where are you?"

From the fourth bed someone screamed, "Eli!" the name dissolving into a sob of pain.

They hurried over to the crowded bed, and Elisha dropped his barbering tools.

Her thick golden hair tangled on the pillow, Helena lay at the outermost. She had flung off the dirty blankets, clutching her bloody gown in a stranglehold as she shrieked. Tears tracked down her face from eyes shut tight. "Nathan! Nathan," she whimpered.

"Here, darling, I'm here." Nathaniel pushed by to grab her hand. "Oh, Love, I'm so sorry."

"Where's the midwife?" Elisha demanded, pulling the blankets down all the way to reveal Helena's perfect legs. He shut his eyes and shook himself.

"Gone," she panted, "physician."

Sister Lucretia shot him a look, her face as grim as his own.

"Sister, we'll need a cart to get the lady home," he told her softly. He needed room to work, and peace, for his sake as well as hers.

Nevertheless, Nathaniel heard him. "You can't think of moving her, not in this condition."

Elisha stared down at his brother, the cacophony of pain beating at him from every side however he tried to ignore it. Beside Helena lay a thin woman, her eyes wide, her skin gray, her mouth stretched open in a final amazement. If Helena stayed here, he had no doubt she would soon look the same.

From the corpse's other side, a girl spoke up through blood-flecked lips. "Can you bring another blanket please? This woman's gone awfully cold."

Through clenched teeth Elisha repeated, "A cart, at once. And the midwife, if you find her."

Lucretia bobbed her head and nimbly hurried off as if she fled the pain around her. Elisha couldn't fathom how she could stand to work there, surrounded every moment by suffering.

Helena screamed again, and Nathaniel stroked the hair back from her sweaty face. "I'm here," he murmured. "And Elisha's come. We'll help you."

Kneeling down by her feet, Elisha shoved back his sleeve, but the examination was unnecessary, for one of the babe's feet could be seen. Jerking back, Elisha flung himself away from the bed. "What the hell were you thinking?" he shouted. Of all the births he'd assisted, this had to be the worst; that it was happening to his own brother's wife was unconscionable. And he knew in his heart that he was to blame. She needed a surgeon's skill and the speed of a racehorse. Skill he had, but speed he had no control over. Even if he ran for the tools he'd need and back again. Better to take her away . . .

"Please, gentlemen, I'll have to ask you to go," said an older nun, bustling up to them as fast as her stout legs could take her. "I am the ward sister here, and you've no—"

"This is her husband," Elisha said shortly. "I'm his brother, a barber and a surgeon."

"Still and all," she huffed, "we are doing what may be done for her. The physician has been sent for."

"Do you think he'll come for her? For any of them?" He waved his arm over the beds.

"The physician is understandably busy, but he is a Christian man."

At Helena's shriek, Elisha cringed. He shoved past the nun and went back to the curtain, his hands balled into fists. The woman had no sense, or at least, no ears. Helena couldn't afford the physician's leisure. Still, he had to control himself, master his own heart before he'd be of any good to her. He started to review what he would need, to picture the tools and where to find them. Already, it was too late to turn the baby against the desperate pressure of the mother's own womb.

"Will the sister bring me a cloth?" asked a timid voice below him, and Elisha turned.

The pale girl with the gashed arm still tried to stop the blood with her hand, watching him from dark and sunken eyes.

Sinking down on the bed beside her, Elisha pulled the towel from his belt and tore it in three. "Give it here," he told her.

Blinking, she glanced away toward the distant nun, then back.

"I'm a barber," he said soothingly. "Give it here, it'll be fine."

Hesitantly, she held out her arm. The gash was long, but not too deep, cutting across the muscles of her forearm. This, at least, he knew exactly how to handle. With the first strip of cloth, he wiped around it. Then holding her hand between his knees, he pressed together the sides of the wound and wrapped it carefully, tucking the bandage end in when he was done. From his ever-present pouch he slipped a packet of white powder and pressed it into her grasp. "Just a pinch for the pain—no more, you hear me?"

"Aye, sir."

"Get out of here," Elisha urged, drawing her up from the bed. "Go home."

With a quick glance behind her, the girl darted away, holding her injured arm close once more. He stared a moment after her, wishing Helena could be so readily healed.

A hand thrust aside the curtain, admitting Sister Lucretia followed by a plump woman with her sleeves bound back from her arms. "Elisha," she grunted. The midwife. Elisha's heart sank yet further when he recognized her: matronly, barely competent, with a demeanor soothing to pregnant women. Her combination of piety and comfort would appeal to his brother almost as much as the fact that Elisha disapproved of her.

Following close, they returned to Helena's side.

"Now, dear," the midwife said, bending down to check the infant's position. Only Elisha caught the flash of horror on her face. When she looked up again, her voice was still as calm as ever, though her hands quavered. "Now, dear, the physician recommends a cutting. We'll lift the babe from your belly and stitch't back up again, eh?"

Nodding desperately, Helena clung to her husband with both hands.

"We'll be needing water then," the midwife went on, "and a better knife than what I've brought."

With a cold certainty, Elisha laid a hand on Helena's taut belly, pressing the still form of the child she carried. Too still. He grabbed the midwife's arm and pulled her aside, turning his face from his brother. "You're going to cut her open?" he whispered urgently.

"The physician advises—"

"He knows who she is, and her circumstances?"

"Aye, Barber, he does," the midwife snapped, tugging at his grip.

Elisha swore under his breath. "So he thinks to save the babe at her expense."

The midwife dropped her gaze, her thin mouth set. "God willing, if I stitch her right up—"

Elisha didn't listen to the rest. Under the best of circumstances, cutting into the abdomen was risky—best left to the master surgeons, and even then more likely to kill than to cure.

He looked at Lucretia.

The nun nodded once. "And horses."

The first good news he'd yet been offered. Elisha grinned. "Bless you."

He lifted Nathaniel to his feet and pushed his barbering tools into his brother's hands. Then, with a nod to the imperious ward sister, he caught up Helena in both arms and drew her to his chest. "There's not a moment to spare."

"But she said—!" Nathaniel began to protest, then he whirled, seizing the midwife's hand. "Come with us."

Elisha met the midwife's eye, the fear in his brother's voice still ringing in his ears. Grudgingly he said, "She'll have need of you."

She held up her hands in a gesture of despair. "Aye, Barber, I'm coming."

"Then we have a life to save," he said, turning away to escape the hospital, and its reeking beds of corpses both living and dead.

"ELISHA BARBER is an edgy, vivid story with engaging characters and a well-drawn setting that's almost, but not quite, our own history. I was drawn right in, quick as a slash of a barber's razor."
-- Kevin J. Anderson, New York Times bestselling author of CLOCKWORK ANGELS

". . . beautifully told, painfully elegant. . ."
--Library Journal starred review

England in the fourteenth century: a land of poverty and opulence, prayer and plague... witchcraft and necromancy.

As a child, Elisha witnessed the burning of a witch outside of London, and saw her transformed into an angel at the moment of her death, though all around him denied this vision. He swore that the next time he might have the chance to bind an angel's wounds, he would be ready. And so he became a barber surgeon, at the lowest ranks of the medical profession, following the only healer's path available to a peasant's son.

Elisha Barber is good at his work, but skill alone cannot protect him. In a single catastrophic day, Elisha's attempt to deliver his brother's child leaves his family ruined, and Elisha himself accused of murder. Then a haughty physician offers him a way out: come serve as a battle surgeon in an unjust war.

Between tending to the wounded soldiers and protecting them from the physicians' experiments, Elisha works night and day. Even so, he soon discovers that he has an affinity for magic, drawn into the world of sorcery by Brigit, a beautiful young witch... who reminds him uncannily of the angel he saw burn.

In the crucible of combat, utterly at the mercy of his capricious superiors, Elisha must attempt to unravel conspiracies both magical and mundane, as well as come to terms with his own disturbing new abilities. But the only things more dangerous than the questions he's asking are the answers he may reveal.

And the adventure continues in
Elisha Magus

You may also enjoy:

The Singer's Crown

Available from Eos Books, wherever books are sold

When his uncle murders his family to take the throne, Prince Kattanan DuRhys is the only royal left alive. . . at a terrible cost. Stripped of his manhood, Kattanan travels as a court singer from one wealthy patron to the next. Given as a courtship gift to the young Princess Melisande, Kattanan feels the stirring of emotions he thought were denied him. But her jealous fiancée has other plans--and the sinister magic to carry them out.

Must Kattanan sacrifice his song to win his kingdom, and the woman he loves?

The Eunuch's Heir

Available in a variety of e-book formats, from
Rocinante

Prince Wolfram of Lochalyn can't possibly live up
to the reputation of his father, the Blessed Rhys, so why
bother to try? Until a series of self-started catastrophes
plunges him into the midst of the growing refugee
population. They claim to be fleeing a war, and only
Wolfram sees the danger that lurks in their mysterious
ways. But his love for an exotic stranger, and his concern
for the princess who pursues him collide with a more
terrible struggle, in which his kingdom may fall and
his very Goddess be brought to Her knees. Discredited
by his past and disdained by his own mother, Wolfram
must find the truth of his birth, and fight to make amends
for all that he's done — or be seduced by the darkness of
distant power.

The Bastard Queen

Available in a variety of e-book formats, from
Rocinante

Beloved bastard of an unloved king, Fiona will do almost anything to please her father, even studying magic though she never shows more than a spark of talent. But the plague that grips their city sends her to work with the dying, as enmity builds between the two peoples her father has brought together. When arson burns a hospital, everyone blames the growing racial tension, until an unexpected suspect comes from the woods on a spirit-quest destined to uncover the secrets of Fiona's past. Then Reynaud, long Fiona's suitor, suddenly asks to marry her sister. Struggling to find a cure for the plague, Fiona becomes ever more convinced that its emergence is no coincidence — and that Reynaud may be leading a conspiracy that will end in genocide.

ALSO BY THE SAME AUTHOR:

Tales of Bladesend

Available in a variety of e-book formats, from
Rocinante

Epic fantasy novellas about heroes who believed the
battle was over.

Winning the Gallows Field

In spite of Trelayne's victories in battle, the road
home is longer than the young knight ever imagined,
and it must begin with rejecting his peasant companion,
Derik, and denying the memory of the half-orc
companion who gave his life for them. Forced to admit
that the battle has changed him, Trelayne tries to be
the champion for the peasantry, only to make things
worse — Derik imprisoned, his betrothed rejecting
him, his war-wounds throbbing. Honor provokes him
to claim a duel with the swordmaster in the hopes of
earning Derik's freedom, but the veterans find that
winning a battle is not the same as winning a war — and
not all demons wear an ugly face.

Joenna's Ax

After Joenna's half-orc son is killed in battle, she disguises herself as a man to join the army and avenge him, adding one notch to the handle of her ax for every demons she kills. But when she volunteers to lead a suicide charge of half-orc scouts, she risks her secret and her own mission to try to save them. Rewarded for her prowess with a grant of land and ownership of her half-orc man-at-arms, Joenna plots to rescue all of the half-orcs from the king's plan to destroy these reviled bastards — making herself a traitor along with them. When their haven is discovered, Joenna leads the half-orcs in a desparate fight against a famous warrior and his knights in the hopes of winning their freedom and claiming their humanity.

ABOUT THE AUTHOR

E. C. Ambrose writes "The Dark Apostle" historical fantasy series about medieval surgery, which began with Elisha Barber (DAW, 2013) and continues with Elisha Magus (July 1, 2014) and Elisha Rex (July 7, 2015). Other published works include "The Romance of Ruins" in Clarkesworld, and "Custom of the Sea," winner of the Tenebris Press Flash Fiction Contest 2012. She is also the author of The Singer's Crown and its sequels, The Eunuch's Heir, and The Bastard Queen, published as by Elaine Isaak. Elaine quite enjoys her alternate identity, aside from a strong desire to start arguments with herself on social media. Under any name, you still do NOT want to be her hero. www.TheDarkApostle.com

In addition to writing, the author works as an adventure guide. Past occupations include founding a wholesale business, selecting stamps for a philatelic company, selling equestrian equipment, and portraying the Easter Bunny on weekends.

She blogs about the intersections between fantasy and history at ecambrose.wordpress.com
and can also be found at facebook.com/
e.c.ambroseauthor
or twitter @ecambrose